SINFUL
ABANDON

JEANNINE COLETTE

Editing and Formatting by Jovana Shirley of
Unforeseen Editing, www.unforeseenediting.com

Printed in the United States of America
First Printing, 2017
ISBN-13: 978-0-9964997-8-1

www.JeannineColette.com

THE ABANDON COLLECTION

A series of stand-alone novels featuring dynamic heroines who have to abandon their reality in order to discover themselves…and love along the way.

Each novel features a new city, couple, and rose of a different color.

Check out these full-length novels in the Abandon Collection.

Pure Abandon

Reckless Abandon

Wild Abandon

Wild Abandon Christmas

To YOU, the reader.
Thank you for giving me a chance.

chapter ONE

Ten p.m., and the only souls in the building are security. They don't look twice as I walk through the lobby of gold and granite, my five-inch stilettos echoing in the vast space. I walk to the elevator and hit the button for my destination.

Jarrod Bellomy.

When the elevator closes, I do a once-over in the reflection of the doors. My sleek brown tresses have been blown out to perfection by my Michigan Avenue hairstylist. My bright brown eyes are lined in ebony and a smoky shadow. My skin is tinted with a touch of bronzer to look sinful, and my lips are barely glossed. They should be since I expect them to be devoured within minutes.

Looking down, I see the beige Chanel trench I purchased at a consignment shop. It's two sizes too big, but who cares? It's Chanel. And, right now, it's hiding a deliciously exotic plum-colored negligee and garters, all picked out to entice the man I've been hunting for the last six months.

Jarrod is my boss and president of the company that owns the lifestyle news program I've been working on for the better part of a year. After my last company—Asher-Marks Communications in New York—closed shop, I found myself looking for work. Not only did my new company have to have a great compensation plan, but it also needed to have the number one thing I was looking for in a job—a rich, single boss.

I found the perfect job and that perfect man in Chicago.

When I took the position, it wasn't just to be a kick-ass producer, overseeing the staff and day-to-day planning of a show that focused on entertainment, gossip, and fashion. I could do that shit in my sleep. Hell, the show was in near ruin when I came on board and turned it around—not that the ungrateful staff cared.

No, my goal was to seduce my forty-year-old boss and one of Chicago's most eligible bachelors. It only took a few months, and here I am, pulling out all the stops in preparation for an engagement.

Growing up with a drunk of a father and a mom who left town would give you life goals like you couldn't believe. Yes, I can and will make my own money. But, since all men are scoundrels, I might as well pick one I can suck every penny out of.

Sounds sad? Yeah, it kinda is. But I don't give a fuck.

Jarrod said he would be working late tonight, so I decided to surprise him with a late-night office rendezvous. If this little act doesn't secure an engagement, I don't know what will.

Dipping my hand inside the trench, I perk my breasts up, making sure they are at full attention. I check my purse to confirm I have the necessary toys for the evening—a blindfold, vibrator, anal beads, and condoms.

The beads are for Jarrod, not me.

He's kind of a freak that way.

The elevator doors open, and I walk toward his office. The newsroom that is usually bustling with activity is eerily quiet. The room is accentuated in gray, the only source of light coming from the streetlights on Wacker Drive. Jarrod's corner office door is closed, the inside light seeping through the bottom of the doorway.

Just outside, I stop for a moment. My hand on the door handle, I take a second to straighten my shoulders and pout my lips. When I walk through these doors, my man is going to fall to his knees, and I am going to let him have me.

Ready for the fun to begin, I open the door, and my body freezes.

My arms fall to the sides.

My purse clangs on the ground.

"Holy shit," I say. I begin to avert my eyes but have to raise my chin again to make sure I'm actually seeing what I think I'm seeing.

"Heather? What are you doing here?" Jarrod asks from his position at his desk where he's standing over Misty Waters, the local weather girl.

Misty is lying on the desk with her bare legs wrapped around Jarrod, her heels digging into his bare ass, as he pumps in and out of her.

Yes, I said that right.

He's still pumping.

"What am *I* doing here? What the hell are *you* doing?" My voice squeaks.

Pants around his ankles, his shirt and tie still intact, Jarrod looks at the weather whore and shrugs. "I was working late, and Misty came by for a break."

"Hi, Heather," Misty says with panting breaths. Her white button-down is undone, exposing a lace bra and double Ds.

"I...you..." My jaw is unhinged, and if I don't get a grip, I'm going to lose every ounce of dignity I have, which is a lot, by the way. "You don't seem upset at all that I'm standing here while you fuck her." My hand is up in the air, palm up.

Still thrusting his pelvis into Misty, Jarrod replies, "I wasn't expecting you. Otherwise, I would have waited. Wanna join?"

The shakes. I get the shakes. My toes start to tremble, and it travels up my calves and into my thighs. My hands start next, and it radiates up through my shoulders, making my head spin.

Do I wanna join?

I mean, if he'd asked if I were up for a threesome, I probably would have been game. My goal is to please Jarrod enough to make him propose. But this? This is blatant cheating. He didn't know I was coming up here. He's banging the freaking local weather whore on his desk. The same desk we've had sex on multiple times.

Throwing my hands up in the air, I spin around and rush back through the newsroom.

"Can you close the door, love? I don't think the cleaning crew would like a show." Jarrod's words echo from his office, but I keep on walking down the corridor and straight to the elevator.

I fold my arms in front of my body and violently tap my foot as I wait for the elevator to open.

Any second now, Jarrod is going to come rushing down the hallway and fall to his knees in apology.

The elevator doors open. I pause for a moment.

Any second now...

The doors are about to close, so I walk inside the cab and press the button to hold the doors open.

Any second...

My heart starts to beat in anticipation. He's probably pulling up his pants right now. I'm sure he's tossing Misty out of his office, and he is going to come rushing after me.

Any...

Oh, fuck it.

I let the doors close and hit the lobby button. That piece of shit isn't coming after me.

What the hell did I expect, chasing after a known womanizer like Jarrod Bellomy? That I'd be the one to make an honest man out of him? What for? It's not like I love him. Hell, I think he's beyond conceited, and he has a terrible personality. But he does have the one thing I'm looking for.

I rush out of the elevator and through the lobby. My heels wobble a little as I try to move out of the building as quickly as possible.

When I get to the sidewalk, I see a taxi and charge for it. *Thank God.* The only thing I want right now is to go home, pour myself a large glass of Tito's, and drown myself in it.

My hand is on the handle. I pull on the lever and open the door when a man's hand charges on top of mine and rips my hand away.

"This is my cab," an irritated male voice says.

I don't even bother to face him. With a hip nudge, I try to force him to the side. "What are you? The taxi police? Get your own fucking cab." I start to open the door further.

He places a hand on the door and slams it closed in front of me.

"What the hell do you think you're doing?" I spin around to face the asshole, and my heart skips a beat.

Standing eye-to-eye with me is a man, a gorgeous-faced man, with cobalt-blue eyes and a sinful mouth accentuated by a masculine jaw and day-old stubble. I am momentarily rendered speechless.

Momentarily.

"Remove your hand from the door."

"In or out, guys," the cabbie calls through the open passenger window.

"I'm getting in as soon as she moves," the man says.

"I got here first. Get your own cab." I pull on the handle, again, but he holds the door closed.

His chest presses into mine. "I did, but you just stole it."

I push back harder. "Stole, my ass. You snooze, you lose."

"I don't care that you're cute and get everything in life. Catch the next one."

If he think's I'm cute, I'll show him just how cute this bitch can be.

Pursing my lips, I dig my heels into the ground. "This has nothing to do with me being a woman!"

"Well, I'd punch you if you were a guy, so let's both be thankful you're a woman."

"I've never—"

"Step back before you get run over," the driver says as he pulls away from the curb.

I jolt back from the car and nearly trip over my stilettos, falling right into the lean, muscular arms of the cab stealer.

"Get off of me," I demand of him even though I'm clinging to his biceps, steadying myself on the blacktop.

Cars are whizzing by us, but all I feel is the curve of his muscle underneath a blue button-down that brings out his eyes. Across his chest is a messenger bag as brown as the perfectly styled hair on his head.

"I'm not touching you." He's not. His arms are out to the sides and in the air to prove it.

Steady on my feet, I brush my hair away from my face and look him in the eyes. "You owe me another taxi."

He rests his head back, looks up to the sky, and lets out a deep breath. "When are you going to see that *I* hailed the taxi? Do you think cabs just show up on curbs when you want them to? Are you a witch with magical powers? If so, please, please, make another one appear. I'd love to see this." His arms are now across his chest, and he's staring me down.

I clench my jaw and level my eyes with his. "You have no clue who you're dealing with. I eat men like you for breakfast."

With a shake of his head, he moves away. "Whatever. Have a good night."

He turns to walk down the sidewalk, and I turn back to the street. I won't lie and say I'm not a little disappointed in his easy retreat. I like a good fight. I'll even give him credit for that punch-in-the-face comment. Now, if he'd actually hit me, that would have been a different story.

As I raise my arm to hail another cab, I feel a tug and a pull backward, and then my too-big trench slips and falls off my shoulders.

"Hot damn, girl." A passerby gawks and whistles at me. "Look at the rack on this one. Didn't know they had call girls up on Wacker. Give us a dance, mama!" His voice is shrill, and he's making obscene hip gestures.

Quickly, I throw my arms across my chest, hiding the very low corset top that has my full breasts pummeling out of the top, my nipples daring to make an appearance.

I spin around to hide the view of my ass cheeks peeking out of the ruffled bottom but have to spin around again to keep the oncoming traffic from witnessing my nearly bare bottom. My upper thighs are fully exposed, and the garters attaching the lace panties to the thigh-high stockings only highlight the creamy flesh.

I'm a free and confident woman. I love to show off my body. But only to those of my choosing. This, being on display for anyone to see is…well, unnerving.

My throat quakes.

My lips tremble.

And the backs of my eyes quiver.

I'm bending down, trying my best to cover my very exposed self, when a warm blanket wraps around me. It doesn't take long to see that the blanket is, in fact, my trench coat, and it is being placed on my shoulders by warm, strong hands.

An arm slings around me, and I am being pulled into a body. I look up to see the side profile of the man I was arguing with over the cab. He's ushering me closer to the curb, his other arm up in the air. He whistles loudly, and a taxi is at the curb in an instant.

With an ease I wasn't expecting, he guides me into the back of the cab. I climb in. When I see his foot step into the car as well, I scoot over and make room.

"Where to?" the cabbie asks.

I look around in bewilderment and swallow. "Lake Shore Drive."

The car starts to move, and I pull my coat tighter around me. Moving to the furthest side of the cab, I look back at the man sharing the bench seat with me.

His mouth is open, ready to speak. "I must have stepped on your belt and dragged your coat as you were walking away. I didn't realize it until I heard that creep making comments."

I shrug with a feeling of disgust. "Not the worst I've heard."

He skeptically eyes me, but I don't elaborate.

I fix my trench and tie the belt back up. Serves me right for having a jacket with no buttons. Thought it would make for a sexy negligee reveal. Not a peep show for all of Chicago.

I run my fingers along the inside of my palm. This night is not turning out how I expected. I was supposed to be getting boinked by a millionaire in a skyscraper. Not ogled by strangers like I'm a two-bit hooker.

Maybe Jarrod is texting me with his apologies. I turn to my bag, but it's not on my shoulder. I feel around the inside of the cab, but it's not here.

"Fuck my life!" I shout into the open air.

"Is there any particular reason we're fucking life right now?" the man asks.

"Not any life. Just my life." I run my hand through my hair. "I left my bag in my office. I must have dropped it when…" I start to say but then realize I'm digressing. "I have no money." I lean forward to the driver. "Let me out. I'll walk."

The car starts to move to the right.

The man next to me throws his arm across my body and says to the driver, "No. Keep driving." Cobalt blues turn to me. "I got this."

I lean back to get a good look at him. He's about my age, mid- to late-twenties. He fills out his button-down well, and his fitted gray trousers showcase his strong thighs. His shoes are brown and generic. No Ferragamos on this guy. His messenger bag has a name I've never heard of, but it looks new.

Despite his designer-free clothing and lack of expensive cologne, he's really good-looking. It's only Sunday night, but he could be out, getting laid by any single gal in Chi-Town. Unless he's gay, which is a possibility.

"Why the hell would you pay for my cab? You were shouting at me a minute ago. Now, you're being…chivalrous?"

He lowers that gaze, sending heat and strength directly to me. "I am not about to let a woman in lingerie and a trench coat walk twenty blocks home, alone, at night in the city."

I scrunch my eyes at him. I don't trust people, especially ones who do nice things for strangers.

"What's your name?" I ask.

"Ryan. What's yours?"

"Heather. Where are you from?"

"Evergreen Park. You?"

"Where the hell is that?"

I know I'm being rude, but he doesn't seem to care because he just laughs lightly and shakes his head.

"You're obviously not from here."

His hand rises to the lever on the ceiling of the cab. The action makes his bicep protrude through his shirtsleeve that is rolled up to his elbows. I can't help but notice the lean muscles of his forearm as well.

"It's a suburb about thirty minutes away."

His words make my eyes flutter up to his face. I blink for a second as I try to recall what he was saying. Or did he just ask me something?

"Queens, New York," I say.

The corners of his mouth rise, as do his brows. "You don't sound like you're from New York. Where's your accent?"

Nice of him to notice. I worked hard to get rid of that dreadful Queens accent. With my dad already the drunken version of Archie Bunker, I refused to bear the nasally tone of my relatives, with each word drawn out way too long. Every time I feel the inflection approach the back of my throat, I snap into action and put my perfect diction back into place.

"I got rid of it," I say matter-of-factly.

This piques Ryan's interest. "How exactly does one get rid of an accent?"

I've never told anyone this because it sounds like the dumbest thing in the world. But, whatever, I don't have to impress this guy. At all.

"Dr. Seuss," I say. When he still stares at me, waiting for me to further explain, I continue, "I used to read Dr. Seuss books as a kid to work on my diction. You'd be surprised by how well it works."

I brace myself for his laughter. Instead, he nods his head and looks back at me, like he's impressed.

I'm suddenly intrigued.

"What's your deal, Ryan from Chicago?"

"My deal? I don't have a deal. Just doing the right thing."

I hate his answer.

"Wouldn't the right thing have been to let me have the cab in the first place? I could have been long gone and out of your life by now."

He smiles a perfect white-toothed grin and speaks with sarcasm, "Yes, but you wouldn't have had any money to pay for your cab. Aren't we lucky that things worked out this way?"

I purse my lips at him but feel my cheeks rise.

Damn him.

The cab pulls up to my building, a gorgeous glass and steel apartment tower. Ryan opens the door and then stands to let me out. When I'm on the sidewalk, I spin around and see he's getting back into the car.

"Don't you want to come up?" I ask him, the breeze off Lake Michigan lifting my hair off my neck.

He stops moving, waits a beat, and then turns around to face me. "Why would I come up?"

My body falls with his peculiar sense of aloofness. "You paid for my cab, so I'm offering to pay you back."

Standing by the open door of the cab, he puts his hand in his pocket. His tousled dark brown hair becoming ruffled in the gentle wind. "I'm not looking for sex."

I roll my eyes to the heavens. "And I'm not offering it to you. Just a drink. I might even have some cash upstairs to pay you back."

He thinks this over for a second.

I find myself growing impatient. "Any minute now."

"How do you know I'm not a serial killer or a rapist?" he asks.

Oh, for the love of Christ.

I walk over to the cabbie and motion for him to lower his window. When he does, I talk to the driver, "I want you to record the time and place of this conversation. My name is Heather McCallister, and this is Ryan..." I pause and then look over to Ryan. "What's your last name?"

"Pierson." His brows are furrowed.

"His name is Ryan Pierson. If I go missing tomorrow or am found hanging in my bathroom, I want you to alert the media that you dropped off a devastatingly beautiful brunette name Heather McCallister at her residence at ten thirty-two in the evening. Got it?"

"The fare is twelve dollars. You gonna pay or what?" The driver sounds very concerned for my safety.

I turn to Ryan for the fare. Instead of handing it over, he just looks at me. It's an odd look, one I'm not used to sharing with men, and quite frankly, it makes me a little uncomfortable.

His eyes are slanted ever so slightly. His brows gently curve in. There's an intensity. A knowing aspect that makes me want to tell him that he knows nothing about me, so he should stop trying to figure me out.

Ryan gives him twenty and then closes the door.

When the two of us are alone on the sidewalk, we stare at each other for a moment. I turn and walk into the building, him following me like some sort of lost puppy.

Charlie, the doorman, is on duty. I pull Ryan by the hand and walk him to Charlie's desk.

Nudging Ryan, I say, "Give him your shoes."

Not asking any questions, Ryan takes off his shoes and hands them to Charlie.

With my hands on the concierge desk, I look at Charlie with a serious expression. "This is Ryan Pierson. You are not allowed to return his shoes until I call from upstairs and say that I am alive and safe. Sound good?"

Not one to argue with me, Charlie takes Ryan's shoes and hands him a valet ticket.

Pulling on Ryan's hand, I drag him to the elevator bank and up to my apartment. With my stilettos on, I'm as tall as he is, giving me the brass balls I need to be commanding over him. For someone who was arguing with me twenty minutes ago, he sure is playing the submissive awfully well.

I open my front door, turn on the light, and let my trench coat fall to the credenza.

"Um, did you mean to do that?" he asks from the threshold.

I raise a bare shoulder and smirk. "You've already seen the goods. What difference does it make now? Want a drink?"

I'm halfway to the minibar when Ryan decides to take a tentative step into my house. I have the tumblers out and the vodka poured when I catch him eyeing up my apartment.

I hand him a glass and hold mine out for a cheers. Our glasses clink.

"Nice place you have here," Ryan says.

"Goes with the package. A woman needs the right aesthetics to attract the right buyer." I take a sip from my glass.

"Are you selling?" he asks. It's somewhat endearing.

"No." I smirk. "I'm in the market for a man. A rich one." As the words come out of my mouth, I think of Jarrod and his pelvic thrusts into Misty Waters.

Oh my God, he was still pumping, even while I was standing there!

I take a deep breath through my nose and blow it out my mouth. Why do I always pick the shittiest men? Last year, I was two years into throwing myself at my last boss, Alexander Asher, only to have the man, who said he would never marry, meet another woman and marry her. She probably drugged him or some other nonsense. For two years, I'd tried to get that guy and nothing, not even a one-night stand.

At least with Jarrod, we've had a relationship. I couldn't tell anyone, of course. He is my boss, and that kind of thing is frowned upon. But, once he proposed, who would care if they fired me? I could find work somewhere else, but I couldn't find another Jarrod.

At least, not another Jarrod with his kind of trust fund.

"You have a CD collection?" Ryan walks over to the entertainment unit and fingers through my music. "I've never met anyone who actually owns CDs."

He's brushing his fingers over the plastic of a Rihanna CD, like it's an artifact. Without asking, he turns on the CD player and puts the disc inside. I haven't listened to this album since college. The Barbadian singer's voice bellows out from the speakers, and Ryan goes back to exploring the room.

He's nice to look at. Tall with a muscular frame that's more lean than bulky, he's strong and secure with a face like a Calvin Klein model. *Man, why do the poor ones always have to be so damn handsome?*

"You don't have any pictures," he states.

I motion to the scenic one above the sofa and wonder how in the world he is missing the giant picture.

"I mean, personal pics, like with friends, family, travel. You know, the kind of pictures people place around their homes?"

"I don't like people, so why would I have pictures of them?"

"Not even your parents?" he asks with the rise of perfect brows.

"My dad sucks, so, no, not even them."

He does another glance around the room. "So, all of these things are just props to attract a wealthy man?"

I raise a finger and give him a wide-eyed and open-mouthed face that says, *Bingo!*

He leans back on his heels and takes a lingering drink from the tumbler, his lush lips kissing the crystal. Those piercing eyes are steady on me. "You ever been in love, Heather?"

"You ever been cheated on, Ryan?" I refill my drink.

"No."

"Of course not. Look at you." I take a fresh sip.

"If you're basing this on beauty, then I can't believe a man would ever be dumb enough to cheat on you." His eyes assess me. No, they appraise me from the tips of my toes, up to my shapely hips, and dip across my swollen breasts, landing on the doe-eyed expression I'm giving him. From the look on his face, he means what he said.

I swallow down any notion of attraction I might have just gotten from that look. "Who said I was cheated on?"

"With that question, you did," he says with a smile.

I hate observant people because you have to watch your every word.

"Shit happens," I say. Then, I raise a finger. "I'm not sleeping with you, so flattery will get you nowhere."

That damn smile widens his face again. He takes a step toward where I'm standing in the middle of the room. "I don't want to go to bed with you. I want to know you."

"Why?"

"I have absolutely no idea, but I'll tell you this." His voice is deep and low. "I've never met a woman like you. You're different from the other girls. I'm hoping you'll tell me enough to quell this aching curiosity inside me."

"Different good or different bad?"

Instead of answering, Ryan moves closer. Our eyes are level, but his body overpowers mine by the energy he's exuding. My insides tingle, and it's the good kind of tingle, the kind that makes me want to unleash my corset and climb the man in front of me like a cheetah in heat.

I inhale a breath and remind myself why I can't be attracted to any ordinary Tom, Dick, or Harry.

Or Ryan, for that matter.

"You have cards?" he asks.

My brows furrow in confusion.

"Blackjack. I'll play you. A win for a sin."

I like this guy. I've been in his presence for under an hour, and I can't get a read on him. It's fun, being kept on my toes.

Placing my drink down on the coffee table, I grab a deck of cards from a nearby drawer, hand it over and take a seat on the couch. Ryan shuffles the deck, like he's a professional dealer, and hands out two cards each.

I hit. He stays.

He wins.

"Why a rich man?" he asks.

He waits for my answer.

"I grew up watching my father have unhealthy relationships with women and alcohol. I escaped my personal hell by reading *People* magazine and watching *Lifestyles of the Rich and Famous*."

"Rich people have problems, too."

"Not money problems. I had a job at ten and paid our rent because the deadbeat would blow all his money. By the time I was sixteen, I moved out and supported myself. Haven't seen him since."

"Where's your dad now?" His interest in my life is uncharacteristic for the men I usually spend my time with.

"Homeless," I state matter-of-factly. "Deal." I wait for him to hand out the cards.

I split a pair and win with twenty to his nineteen.

"First time following a woman home?" I ask.

"First time she was wearing lingerie," he says as a joke.

I raise a brow at him.

"Yes, this is my first time. I wouldn't say, I followed you home as much as you pulled me in."

Ryan deals, and I win again.

I always judge a man by how he answers this question. "How many women have you left the morning after?"

He doesn't blanch at my question. "Two. A howler and a biter."

Honest and without conceit.

He wins the next deal. "Worst thing you've ever done to a person?"

"Sabotage their career. Don't look at me like that. It's a cutthroat world for a woman, and I'll take down anyone in my way."

"A woman taking down a man in the corporate world is impressive, if not scary."

I tweak my mouth in mild embarrassment. "It was a secretary. She was encroaching on my position. I tried to push her back down the totem pole."

Ryan whistles through his teeth. "Damn. Remind me never to get on your bad side."

"You threatened to punch me over a cab!"

"Only if you were a man." He deals and wins again, getting blackjack. "Something you hate but pretend to like?"

"People," I answer.

He looks back at me like that was obvious. He's right. I told him earlier that I don't like people.

I don't know. *What else do I pretend to like?* "Coffee. I drink it because everyone wants to meet for coffee, but it's pretty gross. And sushi. It's so popular right now. Everyone wants to have business meetings over Asian fusion, but I really just want a pizza." My mouth waters at the thought. I haven't had good pizza in forever.

"I'll have to take you to Giordano's then. You'll love it."

The way he says it—as if he is actually going to be back here, taking me out for deep dish—makes my stomach flutter. I dig my nail into my thumb to bring myself back to reality.

"What are you hiding?" I ask. He hasn't dealt the cards again, but I ask anyway, "What's the one thing that would make me hate you as a person?"

Please say you killed someone, stole money from your grandmother, cheated on your wife...

"I get terrible road rage. Bad. You'll want to throw me out," he answers as he deals the cards again.

"That's it?" I lean forward and ask incredulously, "Never stabbed anyone in the back? Taken a bro's girl? Cheated on an exam? Taken steroids? Lied to a boss about your abilities?" I'm fishing for something, anything.

"No. Sorry to disappoint. Were you looking for a bad boy? I do have a temper though. You saw it on Wacker. Sorry about that, by the way. I'd never hit a girl or anything. I just get heated. I played football, and the adrenaline rush is still lingering under my skin."

I stare back at him and wonder why a handsome man with few flaws, minus a temper over hailing cabs, has to wear generic clothing and come from a suburb in Chicago. "I hate you, and I hardly know you."

"You hate everyone," he says. "This is a good song. Wanna dance?"

Ryan stands and raises the volume on the stereo. His hips sway from side to side as he moves to the music. He must have an incredibly low tolerance for vodka because I've never seen anyone actually dance like no one is watching. Plus, I am, in fact, sitting here, watching him dance in my living room.

He leans down and offers me his hands. I scrunch my face at him. *I think I've let a drug addict into my home.*

"You don't dance?" he asks.

With a slow shake of my head, I say, "Not with strangers. Not to old-school Rihanna. And not on my shag carpet."

He quirks up a grin. "So, you don't have a problem with letting strangers come up to your apartment, play CDs on your ancient stereo, and drink with you on said shag carpet, but you do have a problem with dancing." His brows lower over his lids. "Interesting."

"Nothing about me is interesting."

"Everything about you is interesting."

I look down at my glass, the ice melting in the clear liquor. *Nothing lasts forever, including this night. I might as well see where it takes me.*

Kicking off my shoes, I rise and let my stockings dig into the plush carpet. As soon as I'm erect, I notice how tall Ryan is. Looking up to him now, I feel dwarfed and vulnerable.

He grabs my waist and pulls me toward him but not in a sexual way. He's pulling me toward him, so we can actually dance in the same vicinity of each other. When I am close enough, he releases me. The chorus kicks in, and so does Ryan. He sings the words to the song. I know them, too, so I dance.

A huge smile christens Ryan's face as he sings. My arms rise above my head, and my toes sweep across the carpet. I'm not so much dancing as I am jumping, but who cares?

I don't.

Ryan doesn't.

It's quite liberating.

My boobs bounce, and my ruffled bottom flounces, yet Ryan doesn't seem to notice. I hold my hand up to my mouth, like it's a microphone, and start lip-synching the words, outstretching my other arm and pointing a finger toward Ryan, as if he is the man the words are meant for. He acts out his hurt expression but keeps dancing. His eyes meet mine, and I find myself lost in them, singing to them and dancing to them. And I like the way it is making me feel.

The song ends, and there is an awkward silence as the track changes. My heart is racing from dancing, and I'm slightly out of breath, but my lips curve into a smile.

When the next song comes on, it's a slow song. Ryan grabs my hand. I don't fight it. Instead, my head lands on the sculpted curve of his chest. My hand clings to his waist, and my other is being tightly held in his. He rests his chin on my head, and the act feels oddly intimate.

For a second, I contemplate pushing him away. This is super weird and uncalled for. Yet, when he snakes his arm fully around my waist, I realize that I've never been held before. Not like this. Not by anyone.

Wrapped in the arms of a stranger, I feel more protected than I ever have in my life. I close my eyes and nestle into his embrace as our feet move in harmony to the music. With my ear to his chest, I can feel his heart beating. At first, it was wild with excitement, but now, it is slow and steady, as content as mine is.

A mirror by the dining area catches my eye, and I see a glimpse of us together. His magnificent body is holding mine, like I'm the most cherished thing in the world. My small frame is nestled into him. His eyes are closed, so I can appreciate his beautiful face—from the perfect slope of his nose to his broad chin and full lips.

Wouldn't it be magnificent if he were actually a rich mogul? I could live with waking up to a face like that every morning. Maybe he moonlights as an ordinary guy in non-designer shoes because he doesn't want to meet a gold digger. Wouldn't that be something?

It's obviously not true, but, hey, a girl can dream, can't she?

The song ends, so Ryan steps back, releasing me from his hold. My skin tingles with goose bumps. There must be a draft in here because I am suddenly cold.

I look up to Ryan, and those cobalt blues are open and bearing down at me.

His hands are raised, as if he wants to reach out and grab me. I take a tentative step forward, inviting him to do so.

His mouth parts slightly, inhaling a breath. A shiver runs down my spine.

His tongue darts out and skims his lower lip. I bite down on mine.

His eyes are on my mouth and then continue to travel to my breasts, which are heaving with anticipation, and further down to the piping of the corset. They stop just at the edge of the ruffled bottom where skin meets garter.

Those dark brows furrow, and his mouth falls.

But then his eyes dart to the side.

With the clearing of his throat, he says, "You must be uncomfortable in that thing. Why don't you change?"

My eyes widen for a second as I try to decipher if he means change into something more comfortable—*wink,*

wink—or if he actually means to change into something more comfortable.

While I'm standing here, deciding if I should get naked or throw on some yoga pants, Ryan backs away and then turns toward the balcony door. When he opens it and steps outside, I come to the conclusion that I should ditch the boudoir ensemble and throw on some sweats.

In my room, I close the door and lean my back against the cool frame. *What the hell is wrong with me?* A man gives me attention for an hour, and suddenly, I'm lowering my standards for a pair of blue eyes and a nice smile.

I toss on black yoga pants and a purple racerback tank. The built-in shelf bra will have to suffice. Grabbing a twenty from my nightstand, I walk out of the room. My plan is to go out there and tell Ryan that it's time for him to leave.

When I open the door and step out onto the veranda, he turns to me. His body, that was leaning on the railing, straightens up. His chin rises, and when his eyes look at my simple outfit, he smiles a grin so endearing, two dimples appear, one on each of his cheeks. The look of appreciation on his face makes me forget what it was exactly I was going to say.

The twenty-dollar bill being scrunched in my hand brings me back to the here and now.

"Thank you for the ride." I motion toward him to take the cash.

Those full lips purse to the side. "I'm not taking your money. It was an honor." He looks over the veranda and onto the city. "Besides, you need the cash to pay for this place. Must cost you a fortune."

He's not lying. The apartment is less than the rent in New York, but so is my salary.

Ryan stretches his hands on the balcony and looks out at the lights of the buildings. For someone who grew up in Chicago, he is staring at it like he's seeing it for the first time.

"I've always dreamed of having a place like this," he says. "Someday. That's the goal, you know. You and me, we're not so different."

I walk up to the balcony and take a spot next to him. "Oh, yeah?"

"Though I don't plan to marry for money. I want to show my parents I can be something spectacular. Take care of them in their old age."

"You have good parents? What's that like?"

"Simple. Fun. Loving. My parents are hardworking, good people, very affectionate, and they believe in love ever after. They expect the best from us."

"You must have been an angelic child."

He lets out a laugh, shaking his head. "I was mischievous. My parents are deaf, so I spent a lot of time trying to get into trouble. I used to climb onto the roof of my house and pretend I was Spider-Man. The problem with having parents who can't hear is that they can feel everything. The single shake of a shingle, and my mom would come running outside to yell at me."

I smile, despite myself. I lean against the rail and inhale the fog rolling off the lake.

"You mentioned your dad, but what about your mom?" he asks with what sounds like honest interest.

"She left." I look out onto the darkness of the lake. "My parents never hugged me. Hell, they never touched each other. Their conversations were usually arguments or, on a special occasion, laughter during a party they were throwing with their boozy friends. Even those ended in arguments though." I pause and look down at my hands. "She used to say that something better was out there. That a man with money and a life was going to take care of her. Can't blame her for leaving. I just always wondered why she hadn't taken me with her."

An uncomfortable silence passes between us. It's uncomfortable because of me. I've never told anyone about my mom, never cared to. Maybe it's because I've never been asked.

I run my hands along the railing and turn to Ryan.

"I'm sorry you had to go through that," he says.

I wave off his sincerity. "No big deal. Made me who I am today. Confident, successful, driven. I can do anything."

"Yes, you can." He turns back to the darkened body of water. "Lake Michigan is beautiful, don't you think?"

"It's all right."

"So big and intimidating. And strong. It has a current many are surprised to see when they visit. They say it looks like the ocean."

I shrug and look out at the lake. I never paid mind to it in the months I've been here.

He leans his body into the rail and stretches out toward me. "But it's just a lake. What you can't see is—far beyond the horizon, further than your eye can see—it touches various lakes and rivers, getting its strength from those around it. Its current stretches all the way down to the Gulf of Mexico." He stands straight and turns his body to me. "You're like the lake. You think you can do it all on your own without love. But, deep down, there is a current inside you that runs rapid, reaching out, flowing into others. You just have to look beyond the horizon to see it."

Raising my chin, I ask, "How do you know so much about love?"

"I told you, my family believes in love ever after." His tone is a hushed whisper.

Something in his voice makes me lose myself.

I fight the feeling.

"It all sounds like rainbows and butterflies, if you ask me." Before he asks me another question, I speak quickly, "How come you can…" I point to my ear.

"Deaf people can have full hearing children. Their loss isn't hereditary. Just a kink in the wiring, I guess. My two sisters can hear, too."

"What are they like?" Even I'm shocked by my interest.

"Andrea is a spitfire, and Aubrie is quiet. They're twins, and they just started their freshman year of college. Looks like I'll be making a few road trips this year to make sure they're on track."

I push out from the ledge and hold my arms out. "Must be a terrible burden, having to go check out the coeds," I tease.

"Nah, I'm done with the young girls. I like a little sophistication. Maybe even a ballsy brunette who isn't afraid to tell it like it is."

The intense heat in his gaze forces me to swallow hard and look away, back at the never-ending lake.

"Well then, you wouldn't have loved me in college. I was a geek. And ugly. Mousy brown hair, acne, and a wardrobe from The Salvation Army. Yeah, I was a sight. That was all before I got ahold of a stylist and aesthetician." I release a hand from the rail and turn toward Ryan, who is looking at my toned legs in confusion. "You're probably wondering when I got hot."

His head tilts to the side, and his eyes squint awkwardly. "Actually, I was thinking you don't have the personality of the girl you described."

I raise a shoulder and say, "I know. I have a crazy amount of confidence."

"Geeky girls are usually funny. You're not very funny."

My eyes dart back to him. "Ryan!"

He holds his hands out in defense. "Honest to God, usually, unattractive girls make up in personality what they lack in looks."

I turn and drum my fingers on the railing. "So, you're saying, I lack personality."

"Not at all." His words are quick. "You're feisty. It's sexy."

My fingers stop strumming. I give him the side eye. I want to smile at his compliment, but it's a stupid compliment, so I don't.

What I would have given to have a guy like Ryan Pierson pay attention to me in college. The hot football player and the drama geek are a couple made in movies, not real life. But, it figures, after a regimen of Proactiv, a box of hair dye, eyebrow threading, and endless amounts of cardio, guys like him pay attention to me. Well, I don't pay attention to them. They're all users. So, I've flipped the tables, and I use them right back.

"I used to be fun," I start, not knowing why I'm sharing this story with him. I can't help myself as I continue, "In grade school, I was voted Miss Funny Pants. I used to write these one-man plays and act them out for my friends. I was really good at impersonations."

"Let me hear one."

"No way."

"Come on. I'll show you mine if you show me yours." He has a twinkle in his eye.

I roll my eyes to the sky. "Okay, you first. What you got?"

With his cheekbones pronounced and a Cheshire Cat grin, he curls his brows down. His chin pops out just slightly as he leans in. With a low, seductive voice, he says, *"In my experience, the prettier a girl is, the more nuts she is, which makes you insane."*

I don't know the line, but I know the actor. "Ryan Gosling."

Ryan breaks character, and that gorgeous smile is back. *"Blue Valentine.* Ever seen it?"

"No, I haven't. But that was very good."

"Your turn." He crosses his arms over his chest and waits for me.

My shoulders fall as I think of what ridiculous impression I'm going to do for this man. "I haven't done this in a long time, so don't judge."

Taking a deep breath, I square my shoulders back and then put my hands up in the air. My eyes bug out, and I open my mouth wide. I make sure my head vibrates as I talk from the back of my throat, as I do my best Kathy Griffin impression. *"My fear of camping: I'm convinced bugs will crawl up my vagina and lay eggs. Isn't everyone?"*

A soft clap pulls me out of character, forcing me to look down and push a rogue hair behind my ear.

"That was awesome," Ryan says in a voice that is not his own. It's excited and rushed. I look up and see him lunging toward me as he talks with his hands out in the air, "That was, like, the best." He takes quick breaks in between each word. His body twitches as he says, "That was the best Kathy Griffin impersonation. Ever!"

A huge laugh escapes my mouth. I lean forward and hold my sides at the worst Jimmy Fallon impression I've ever seen.

"What? That was good, no?"

Still trying to catch my breath, I stand up and use my sexy Colombian accent when I say, *"In my country, if you want to do an impression, you have to do it right or else you'll get your head cut off by the drug lords."*

Ryan's face is practically beaming. "That was the most amazing Sofía Vergara I've ever seen." He points a finger at me. "You practice when no one is watching."

I want to make a face and tell him he's crazy. With a closed-mouth smile, I nod my head and look down at my feet.

When I raise my eyes, I notice that Ryan is no longer laughing. He's staring at me like he's just realized something. I tilt my head in question.

"You're amazing," he says, his voice deep, sensual. "Funny. Beautiful. You should laugh more often."

His words take my breath away.

"I suppose I could use some clever in my life. And charming," I reply, my eyes not leaving his.

"So, you think I'm clever and charming?"

"Pfft. I was talking about Charlie the doorman," I tease.

Ryan charges after me and tickles my sides. I laugh hysterically and curl my body in, retreating backward from the onslaught of affection. I haven't been tickled in...ever.

My back hits the outside wall of my apartment. The stucco is rubbing against my back, yet all I can feel is the hard, hot male against my chest. His hands are molded into my ribs, his legs entwined with mine.

He's still. So still. My laughter dies down, and in its place is anticipation. I'm yearning for what those cobalt-blue eyes gazing down on me are about to do.

"I'm going to kiss you now." It's not a request. It's a warning.

With sinful abandon, he kisses me, a stranger he met an hour ago on a busy street and followed to her apartment.

Letting go of every inhibition, I let him.

I part my lips and let his tongue enter my mouth. Soft, sensual lips devour mine in a way I've never been kissed before. They're claiming me with lust and need but also with desire and obsession.

His hands dig deeper into my sides. I raise mine and run them through the smooth tendrils of his dark hair. His mouth traces my jaw and moves down the skin of my neck. When he reaches the spot just below my ear, I moan in expletives.

Ryan's hands rise to my head, his fingers lacing through my hair. He reclaims my mouth, and I melt into him. His body has to slightly lean down, and I wrap a leg around his torso. Our bodies become one of molten heat, and the heavy weight of his intense erection is pressed against the sweetest spot on my body.

Needing more, I raise my other leg and climb him. He takes my weight, like it's nothing. With one hand on my ass and the other cradling the back of my neck, Ryan walks us through the balcony door, which he kicks closed with his foot.

For someone who has never been to my place before, he easily finds the bedroom. Without releasing me, he takes a seat on the bed. My body straddles him with familiarity.

It's like I know this body.

I know this man.

"Fuck," he breathes as my core rubs up and down, the hard steel threatening to release from the wool fabric.

My breasts are alive, tickling with need. I need them to be touched, tweaked, kissed.

My tank top is off, and Ryan wastes no time in lowering that incredible mouth. With one lash of his tongue, I let out a groan. He does it again, raising his other hand to pinch the neglected nipple.

Men don't pay attention to breasts like they used to. The art of foreplay has gone out the window, everyone looking for a quick blow and a bang.

But not with Ryan.

Keeping the steady glide of my hips, I slide against his cock, my clit throbbing. Ryan's head falls back, and a beautiful sigh escapes his mouth. I'm doing this to him with his clothes on. I can't wait to see how he responds when they're off.

One by one, I undo the buttons of his shirt. Satin skin is exposed with each opening until a taut, defined chest and torso are on full display. He's virtually hairless, except for a light sprinkling of hair leading down from his well-defined stomach.

I run my fingers over his pecs and go into sensory overload. He's so hard and soft at the same time. If I could figure out a way to get closer to him, I would.

With my lips, I kiss down his neck.

With my tongue, I navigate the planes of his body.

With my hands, I unfasten the belt and button of his pants.

With my eyes, I take in his massive erection, large, thick, and ready for the taking.

And, with my mouth, I devour every inch of it.

"Heather," he growls when my tongue dances up and down the pleasure vein and twirls around the swollen head.

He leans back on his forearms and intently watches me. I hold his gaze and make an imprint in my mind of this gorgeous male with satin skin and hard muscles. His mouth forms an O, breathing in short breaths over the movements of my mouth.

His balls are tight as I caress them with my hand. I want to give him the most insane blow job he's ever had. I have a plethora of sex toys, but they've all been used before.

Out of the corner of my eye, I see an elastic hairband.

Ryan lets out a groan when I sit back on my heels to reach over for the hair tie. Using two hands, I make it as large as I can and slide it over and down the shaft before going lower and under his balls.

"Did you just MacGyver a cock ring?" he asks.

I laugh at his reference. "Yes. Yes, I did."

"You're full of surprises," he says.

His eyes are carnal, despite the grin on his face. The piercing deep, dark cobalt takes my breath away.

"You have no idea," is all I say before I dive back and take his cock so far deep into my mouth, it hits the back wall of my throat.

Pumping the base with my hand, I lap and suck him down. His head falls back, and he breathes out a series of the sweetest curses. My jaw is tight, but each glorious sound of his breath makes me want to push harder. I've never enjoyed going down on a man as much as I am right now.

Ryan leans up on the bed. His fingers lightly caress my head. He's not bearing down, forcing his weight on me. No, he's gently guiding me, assisting me.

"I'm going to come," he warns, gesturing with his fingers for me to lift my mouth.

I go down on him faster, letting him know I want every drop. And when he comes, it's with a deep growl, and I swallow every salty piece of him.

Leaning back on the heels of my feet, I watch a panting Ryan. While I enjoyed giving him pleasure, I'm internally kicking myself for letting him finish. Now, the party's over. He won't stick around to take care of me.

I carefully remove the hair tie and then rise to my feet, grabbing my tank from the bed.

"What are you doing?" he asks.

"Getting dressed."

"Oh no, you don't." Ryan grabs my hips and pulls me toward the bed.

In one stealthy movement, he flips me onto my back, his body over me. He kicks his pants off, that incredible physique now fully exposed. Ripping the tank from my hand, he throws it onto the floor and kisses me hard on the mouth, no care in the world that I taste of him.

His hands hold me tight. His hips rock against me.

My head spins at the thought of how fast he's gotten hard again.

"Did you think I wouldn't want to repay the favor?" he whispers into my ear before taking a nip on the lobe.

An electric current shoots to my head. His mouth on my neck is intoxicating.

"I wasn't playing tit for tat."

Ryan lifts his head. "That sounds dirty."

My head falls to the side as I laugh. "You're twelve."

"I had your tits, and now, I want your tat," he says as his hand snakes over my pants and rubs my clit up and down.

I groan, despite his incredibly corny line.

"If you think I'm the kinda guy who would let a beautiful woman suck my dick and not return the favor, then you have me all wrong." His thumbs hook into the sides of my pants, and he lowers them over my hips. As his fingers travel, so does his mouth, slowly down my body. "Not only am I going to lick your sweet pussy until you're screaming my name," he says, throwing my pants to the ground, "I am also going to fuck you until the sun comes up."

His mouth is hovering over my core. My hips buck in desperate need to be touched.

"And what if I don't want to be fucked?" I ask.

His tongue darts out and takes a swipe over my clit. The sensation ripples up my body, and my hips jolt further off the bed.

"Then, I'll leave." He places his hands on my thighs, holding them wide and in place as he licks again.

My fingers dig into the thousand thread count sheets.

"I don't want you to leave," I breathe.

With a grin, he looks up at me and says, "Good, because I have been dying to touch you since you tried to steal my cab."

"It wasn't your—" My words are swallowed by my inhale when Ryan goes back down and licks my clit again.

This time, he doesn't stop.

His tongue is unlike anything I've ever felt. With every swipe, my desire builds. My fingers run through his hair. When he dips a finger and caresses me from the inside, I grab my own hair and scream out.

The act only makes Ryan continue on. His tongue is firm and fast, unrelenting. When I look down at him, the sight only makes me burn further with need.

I have a terrible confession to make. I've never come from a man going down on me. It takes me forever, so I cut the act short and jump right into sex. But this feeling burning through me, this build happening inside—paired with the sensation of his hands on my thighs, his mouth moving with vigor, and the groans of satisfaction he gives with every cry from my mouth—makes me lose myself in the moment.

"Touch yourself," he moans, his hands and mouth still on me.

I lower my hands to my breasts and circle my nipples. It's exactly what I need to send me over the edge. The sensations are exquisite. The desire builds higher and stronger inside me. I close my eyes and arch my back. My body ignites, and as he sucks on my clit one more time, I explode, screaming his name into the dead of night.

My core throbs and pulses, tightening with the intense orgasm.

Ryan doesn't stop. He takes me through the waves and doesn't relent until my body sinks into the bed with erratic breaths.

I raise my hands above my head and enjoy the post-orgasmic bliss.

My first oral orgasm. It only took thirty-one years.

Ryan climbs up my body and holds himself up at arm's length. "Should I go now?"

His words force my eyes open, and I see a devilish gleam.

"Hell no." I wrap my arms around his neck and pull him down to me.

His throbbing erection sinks into my thigh, but he makes no move to enter. Instead, he kisses me. These kisses aren't the rushed movements of someone who wants to get in and get out. No, he kisses me like the act is more sensual and orgasmic than anything else we've done so far tonight.

His mouth is slow, purposeful.

With our lips still attached, Ryan lies down on his side, pulling me into him. Our lips and tongues fall into the dark abyss. While his hand is in my hair and the other is on my hip, my hands wander over his body, feeling every curve and delicious indent. His mouth moves to my jaw and neck, and when he comes back to my mouth, I realize that I missed his lips, even for those brief seconds.

And just knowing that his swollen cock is inches from my needy core is making me desperate for him to be deep inside me.

I roll to my side. My hand hovers over the handle of my nightstand.

What must he think of me? How we met, what I was wearing, where we are now? I make no excuses for my lifestyle. I don't regret my decisions. Yet I don't want Ryan to think I am someone who just has sex with anyone. If I open this drawer and he sees what's inside, will he think less of me?

A soft kiss on my shoulder gets my attention. That sweet gesture is overwhelming.

"Hey," he says, his hand under my chin, forcing me around. His knuckle caresses my face. "In my pocket is my wallet. It's smart to always be prepared."

My head falls onto his shoulder, and a slight smile lifts my face. I nod and then roll over. I grab his pants off the floor. I hand him his wallet and watch as he pulls the condom out and sheaths himself in it.

"Turn around."

I do as he says.

With my back to him, Ryan slides an arm under my neck. His other arm lifts my leg up and over his outer thigh. He guides himself inside me from behind. When he is fully in, we both cry out. Wrapping his hand around my lower stomach, he pumps in and out in intense, controlled movements. His hips roll into me, hitting the very sensitive spot no man has ever cared to claim.

"I need you," he says, pulling my head toward him.

And I need him, too. Not until this moment did I know how lonely my life has been.

He kisses me, holding me, grinding deep into me.

I let him touch me.

I let him caress me.

I let him love me like I've never been loved before.

The level of intimacy is sweet.

It's empowering.

It's sexy.

It's erotic as sin.

chapter TWO

The early morning sunlight casts its rays through the blinds while the sound of my alarm wakes me up. Naked and draped in white sheets, I roll over to turn it off.

My body is sated. Ryan made good on his word and made love to me until the sun came up. That was only two hours ago.

I roll over and feel an empty side of the bed.

Where he should be is a note and a lavender rose. I lift the flower to my nose and inhale the scent. It's nothing compared to the smell of him in my arms.

> *Heather,*
>
> *I would have made you breakfast in bed, but I had to be at work. Lucky for me, the bakery on the corner was open. Since you don't like coffee and you're from New York, I took a chance on tea and a bagel. Tonight, you can tell me if I was right.*
>
> *I'll be here at eight.*
>
> *Ryan*
>
> *P.S. Since you weren't up to vouch for your safety, I am walking around the streets of Chicago, shoeless.*

The biggest grin is on my face right now. He's funny and charming and hot as hell.

Looking on my nightstand, I see the pastry bag and a to-go cup. I feel like I've hit the jackpot with this one.

Jackpot.

My shoulders fall as I blow all the excitement out of my lungs. A jackpot is the one thing Ryan doesn't have. I won't lie to myself and say it doesn't bother me. I really like him.

Fine, I know. I know nothing about him. Yet just the thought of him makes me smile, and that's gotta count for something, right?

Running the petals of the rose across my face, I close my eyes and think of him. Dark hair, blue eyes, and a mouth that was made for loving...

Yeah, I've got it bad.

I get up and start to get ready. In the shower, I think of Ryan's hands on me. As I blow out my hair, I think of his hands wrapped in it as he kissed me. When I get dressed, I think of what I should wear when I see him later tonight.

I pull out a lavender dress to match the rose. I'm being corny. And you know what? I like corny.

"Why are you smiling?" Meg asks suspiciously from her place at her desk.

"Any calls?" I ask, ignoring her peaked eyebrows from behind the thick red frames of her glasses.

"Uh, yeah." She fumbles nervously around her desk, her brown ponytail swaying with the movement.

I start to walk to my office.

When she finds the notepad, she gets up and follows me down the hall. Holding up the notebook, she speaks quickly, "Bruce from CAA confirmed the appointment for next Thursday, Sheryl from props wants to talk to you about the budget for the summer fun demo, and Jarrod is waiting for you in your office."

She says that last line as I open my office door and see the dark skin and lightly salt and peppered hair of the two-timing desire of my yesterday's affection.

Jarrod rises and holds out his hands. "Heather, you're late."

"I know." I walk past him and around to my desk.

Meg is still standing in the doorway.

I raise my hand and shoo her away. "That's all." Then, I turn my attention to Jarrod and shoo him away, too.

He feigns a hurt expression. "Baby, you're not upset about last night, are you?"

Turning on my computer, I click the mouse, pretending to be intrigued by what is on the screen.

"Let me make it up to you." He places a hand inside his lapel and produces a long and thin velvet box, probably containing a bracelet.

"When did you get that?" I ask.

"Does it matter?"

I look around and wonder how I was ever attracted to such a vile man. Okay, I know why I was attracted to him, but his utter lack of concern about this situation is making me cringe.

I lean back in my chair and fold my arms. "Do you keep I'm-sorry jewelry on standby?"

He steps backward and appraises me. His eyes crease. "What's gotten into you?"

I blink a few times, trying to decide if he's being facetious. "You were fucking Misty Waters on your desk."

His mouth purses as his head tilts. That rise of his brows, acting like he doesn't see the problem, makes my eyes bug out.

"Heather, I think you might be confused as to what kind of relationship this is. I want you. I plan to make this official. We've spoken of that. But I don't plan on giving up other women. If we are going to make this work, then you need to understand that."

"By official, you mean…"

"Marriage. I'm forty years old. It's time I started a family. You're young and beautiful. You understand my business and appeal to me in every way." He steps around the side of my desk, taking a seat in front of me. Placing the velvet box on his lap, Jarrod leans into me and explains, "I plan on marrying only once. I don't like divorce. They're messy, and frankly, I don't like parting with money." His straight face lets me know he's not kidding. "You will want for nothing for the rest of your life. And neither will I."

He opens the box. Inside is a bracelet of diamonds and rubies. The stones glisten, even in the terrible overhead lighting of my office.

As beautiful as the bracelet is, I turn my attention away and up to Jarrod. "Let me get this straight. I can be your wife, but you will also be with other women. Does that mean I can be with other men?"

The velvet box snaps shut.

"There will be a prenup in place. You stray, you pay."

My stomach falters. I hate the way my conscience is making an appearance right now.

"Why do you want to marry me if I'm not enough?"

He leans in and places a kiss on my cheek. "Because, my darling, you and I only care about one thing. I can't marry someone who loves me. I need someone who loves my money."

Had the proposal presented itself yesterday, I would have said yes.

Today, something feels wrong.

"I don't think I can. Things have"—I pause, looking for the right word—"changed."

He sits back and studies me for a moment. This conversation is not going as he expected. "Your loss." He stands up, taking the bracelet with him, and walks to my doorway. His body stills and then turns around. "Something happened, and it has nothing to do with Misty Waters. I have a feeling, you'll change your mind."

When he is gone, my head falls to my desk, and I lightly bang it on the wood. The sight of my lavender dress catches my attention, and I shake my head.

And then I bang my head again on the wood.

Spinning around on my desk chair, I look out the window at Chicagoland. It's a unique city with a river that runs through it. Large steel structures, immense in power and integrity, are separated by the Chicago River that winds its turquoise beauty between the coldness of the city, bringing light and beauty into it.

I feel a simmer under my skin. The blood flowing freely through my heart is just like the river that flows into the lake.

How can I be falling for this guy so hard, so fast?

"You'd better be worth it, Ryan Pierson," I say to myself with a sigh.

"Heather?" Meg is knocking at my door. She pops her head in. "Here are your notes for the production meeting."

Good. Work. I need something to distract me from the inner turmoil of my subconscious.

Taking the folder from Meg, I walk down the hall, and she follows me. When I get to the conference room, I walk into the full room, passing the employees I have no interest in ever socializing with, and take my seat on the right, next to where Jarrod sits. Meg sits behind me in a chair against the wall. I need her close, so I can beckon orders to her at my will.

I open my folder and get ready for the meeting.

Jarrod walks in and starts with the numbers for last week's ratings, putting a spin on them to make them sound better than they actually are. Everyone claps at the show's success. I roll my eyes.

Next, we go over the afternoon broadcast and talk about the planning, segment for segment. I have a problem with everyone's assignment and raise my hand in question of each.

The beauty of Jarrod is that he and I think the same way. That's what attracted him to me in the first place. He likes the way I command the room and thinks I have excellent production skills.

When the show is mapped out and my critiques are delivered, he turns his attention to the last order of business of the morning. "Before we go, we have some new blood in

37

the room. Our fall interns start today. Why don't you guys stand and tell everyone who you are? Make it quick though. We have a show to run."

I take a moment to answer emails on my phone as the young twenty-somethings rise from their seats and awkwardly introduce themselves.

Ashley from the University of Illinois tells us she's a communications major, her voice squeaking, and she wants to be a reporter.

Don't they all?

Max is a junior at Loyola. This is his fourth internship in two years. He's obviously the overachiever in the group. And, Zahara, from some school I've never heard of, is just super excited to be here.

I click on an email and answer it.

"Last but not least, who are you?" Jarrod asks, clearly as interested in getting this meeting over with as I am.

"Ryan. I'm a senior at Northeastern."

I must have had too much tea this morning because my heart rate speeds up.

There's an awkward pause, which I appreciate, because I can answer this email in silence.

"Do you have a last name?" Jarrod asks.

This guy must be nervous as hell. I click Send and tap on the next email to answer it.

"Pierson. My name is Ryan Pierson."

My thumb stops moving. I don't want to look up. I can't because, deep down, I know that the Ryan Pierson standing on the other side of the room is the same man who I wore a lavender dress for.

When I venture the nerve to look up, my heart drops. Standing in a white shirt and navy pants, wearing a tie that looks like his mom bought it for him, is my Ryan. He's looking straight at Jarrod.

"You're a strong-looking lad. Football?" Jarrod asks.

Of all the people to take an interest in, he chooses Ryan?

"Yes, sir. Achilles injury ended my season. Don't think I'll be playing out the last year."

I hate that he called Jarrod sir.

"Sports journalism is your game then," Jarrod says. "You know, we don't cover sports on this show."

"I was late to the internship process. You were my only choice."

I turn to Jarrod, expecting him to be insulted by Ryan's words.

Instead, he laughs and rises from the table. Pointing to Ryan, he says, "I like you, kid." To everyone else, he says, "That's all for today."

Jarrod walks out of the room, and everyone files out.

Including me.

Hauling ass, I fumble in the hallway when I see Ryan behind me.

An intern?

College?

Oh God, does this mean I slept with a teenager?

I falter on my heels, hooking a right down the hallway, and dart into a darkened room, slamming the door behind me. As soon as my back hits the wall, I cringe at the thought that I just slammed myself into the copy room.

I can't believe my luck. For the first time in forever, I actually feel something for someone, and he turns out to be the freaking intern. And, to imagine, I refused a million-dollar proposal for someone who probably still lives with his mom.

I think I'm going to be sick.

"Heather, I know you're in there." Ryan's voice echoes from the other side of the door.

I can't have him making a scene, calling out my name from the hallway. If anyone learns of our secret affair, I'm fucked.

I open the door, do a quick look right and left to ensure the coast is clear, and then yank Ryan by the tie, hurling him inside the room.

"College?" My voice is low but harsh.

Ryan curiously eyes me, surprised by my reaction.

"Yes," he says cautiously. "How old did you think I was?"

I slam my hand to my forehead. "I don't know. Twenty-seven, twenty-eight…"

"Twenty-one," he verifies.

My hands fly wildly up in the air. "Well, at least you're able to drink. I can strike aiding and abetting a minor off my list of horrors."

His head tilts to the side. "Are you…mad?"

Am I mad? Is he kidding me? How did he think I would react when I found out he was still in the days of beer pong and frat parties?

"You're a child, Ryan. Don't you think that's something you should have brought up last night?"

"A child?" he stammers, unhappy with the label. "Are you fucking kidding me right now?"

I motion for him to be quiet. I don't need the whole office hearing this conversation.

Ryan is having none of it. "You didn't think I was a child last night when I was sucking on your clit."

His words knock the wind out of my system. "No one can find out about last night. If Jarrod—"

"Is that who you were here to seduce last night? Jarrod Bellomy?" He says Jarrod's name like it's the vilest thing in the world. "Help me understand this. It's okay to fuck the boss, but you're embarrassed by the intern."

His face is a sneer, so different from the man I was with last night.

He leans back on his heels, his chin rising a touch. "I get it. No, it's not really an age thing or even a position thing. Let me ask you, Heather, what would you think of me if I told you I had millions just waiting for me in a trust fund when I graduate?"

He moves toward me, that incredible frame of his towering over me. His hard muscles are defined through the crisp white shirt. He pins me with his hips against the copy machine and lifts me in one swift motion. "If I were loaded, filthy fucking rich, would you think of me as a boy"—he pushes his groin into me, and I gasp as his powerful erection presses hard against the apex of my thighs—"or a man?"

On instinct, I swing a leg around his hip. The feeling of him on top of me is so familiar, so right. He runs the tip of his nose up mine and threatens me with a kiss. My mouth parts as he draws closer and away. Closer and away. He's teasing me, tempting me with the thought of feeling his mouth on mine again.

I raise my arms to put them on him, anywhere, somewhere, but they're halted midair when he catches them by the wrists and holds them away from him.

His body tenses beneath my leg. My eyes open to see the cobalt hot with anger.

"Too bad I don't have a goddamn pot to piss in." He throws my arms down and steps back. His jaw is clenched.

If he could spit on me, I'm sure he would.

I take a few shaky breaths. "You have it all wrong. This has nothing to do with money. I woke up this morning, and I was the happiest I've been in years." I can't believe how things have changed. "I broke up with Jarrod. I wanted to see where this thing would take us."

A deep breath escapes his lips, and with it, some of the anger also leaves his eyes. He takes a step back toward me, the beautiful smile I saw last night back on his lips. "Then, let's see where this thing takes us."

"No." I hold out my hand, halting him from coming too close.

He furrows his brows and looks away. He knows exactly what I am going to say.

"You're still my intern."

"I'll give it up."

"You're only twenty-one, Ryan. Your twenties are for screwing anything that moves. Not shacking up with someone who's a decade older than you. You're supposed to date around and find out who you really like. Find out who you are. You're so young. You don't know what's out there."

I think my soft speech has kicked some sense into him.

For a hot second.

Ryan bites his lip and curses into the darkened room. "You think I'm too young to know what I want? I got news for you, Heather. I know more about life and love at twenty-one than you'll know at forty. Because I let myself feel things, and I don't put a label on people."

He points a finger at me, and suddenly, I feel like the child in this situation.

"I know who I am, and I know what I want. I can't believe I started my day off finally thinking I found the woman of my dreams. More like a fucking nightmare." He hisses as he opens the door. Just as he's about to leave, he turns and adds, "Nice dress."

With the slam of the door, my heart jolts.

Clenching my eyes tight, I try to quell the tears threatening to burn down my cheeks. I refuse to cry over a man, especially one I've only known for a few hours.

Turning the pain into something more useful, I straighten my dress, wipe the undersides of my eyes, and storm out of the copy room and down to Jarrod's office, passing the secretary while she's motioning to me that he's on a call.

Opening the door, I stop for a second, allowing him to adjust to the fact that I just barged into his office.

Jarrod holds the phone to his mouth. "Hold on one second," he says to the caller. He puts the phone to his chest.

"Five carats," I say. "As your wife, I refuse to wear anything less than that."

Bless me, Father, for I have sinned.

I just sold my soul to the devil.

chapter THREE

I'm being very New York today. Black dress, black heels, black sunglasses, and my hair is pinned high in a bun fit for a ballerina. I look like Audrey Hepburn going to Tiffany's, but I feel like I'm going to a funeral.

After drinking my weight in Tito's—on an empty stomach, mind you—I found myself dancing in my living room to late nineties pop, and I might have started crying when an NSync ballad started playing.

"Morning, Heather." Meg's voice trails off as I saunter past her, not even taking off my sunglasses. She's up from her desk in record speed, adjusting those red-rimmed glasses as she follows me. "I have your notes for the pitch meeting, your noon lunch was canceled, and Jarrod was here this morning."

I open the door and see a small black bag with gold writing on my desk. I reach back and take the folder from Meg's hands without looking in her direction. I'm staring at the bag when I hear the door close behind me.

I take off my sunglasses and continue to stare.

Walking over to the desk, I peer inside. A black box is in there. Dipping my hand inside, I pull out the box, open it, and procure another box. This time, it's velvet.

"Holy shit," are the words that pour out of my mouth when I open the box and see the massive rock sitting on the velvet cushion. I hold the box up to the light and tilt it in the air, letting the light reflect off the five-carat brilliant cut round diamond engagement ring sitting on a band of pave diamonds.

It's not exactly the proposal all girls dream of, but it's certainly the one I asked for.

I slide the ring onto my finger and am instantly weighed down by the size of it. My hand and heart have never felt heavier.

Why did I tell Jarrod I wanted a ring? Why did I say anything?

Putting this ring on proves that I am everything Ryan accused me of being.

I bang my fist on the wall. *Why do I, all of sudden, have to have a conscience about the matter?*

Ryan acts like he knows the ways of the world. He doesn't know what it's like to be dirt poor. To have to steal groceries at ten years old, so you have something to eat. And then come home to have your dad and his woman of the night take them from you.

I give Ryan ten more years, and he'll be a womanizer like the rest of them. He'll be cheating on his girlfriend or wife. Maybe he'll be an elusive cad, a lothario who strings women along, only to ditch them for another. Men only care about two things—their dicks and their wallets. The smaller one is, the bigger the other one seems to get.

And Ryan has a small wallet.

I bang my fist on the wall again.

Just because he is an exceptional lover does not mean he's worth changing my plans and my lifestyle. Ryan thinks I don't know a thing about love. Maybe I don't. What I *do* know is a lot about lust, and what we shared the other night was pure, unadulterated lust.

And why am I worrying so much about what the kid thinks? I should be worried about what my colleagues might think. They've been whispering about me for months, excluding me from their camaraderie. People aren't stupid. They know I've been sleeping with the boss. I've just been too good at hiding the evidence, so they couldn't prove anything. Especially now that Jarrod and I are engaged. We're in love.

At least in their eyes, we are.

I look out my office window to the slimy green waterway that sits in between buildings, imposing on the city and making it impossible to get across town without having to cross one of the ridiculous bridges.

Let me tell you something about the Chicago River in the summer. It smells like rotten eggs.

I saunter into the conference room and take my seat.

Ryan is seated at a chair along the wall on the opposite side of the room. Children aren't allowed at the big kid's table.

His head is down, as he's scouring over notes on a legal pad. His brown hair is brushed back, the ends a touch too long. He's wearing a blue-and-white-checkered shirt and khaki pants along with metal-framed glasses that cause me to let out an internal groan. *Of course he has the sexy Clark Kent thing going on.*

As if he can feel my stare, Ryan lifts his head. Those blue eyes connect with mine. My breath hitches, and for a second, I can't think of anything but the desire to crawl across this table and mount myself on top of him.

His chest puffs out. His tongue skims his bottom lip.

My mouth parts, and while I'm actually contemplating asking him to move to my side of the room, I see his gaze sweep down my neck to the scoop of my dress and then over to the slope of my arm before crashing on the ring on my finger.

His eyes turn dark. His face pulls in. Vileness and disgust are written all over that beautiful face.

I flip the stone around, so it's nestled inside my palm, and I open my folder.

I don't have time to be judged.

"Morning, people." Jarrod walks in. He stops at the head of the table and throws his books, papers, and phone down. Adjusting the button on his jacket, he takes a seat and rifles through his things as he starts the meeting.

He takes his time with working his way around the table, listening to everyone pitch him their story ideas. All the while, I sit and wait for him to look my way, curious to see if I am wearing his ring.

"Ryan Pierson, star athlete, what do you have for me?" Jarrod says, bringing Ryan to attention.

He holds out his yellow pad, glancing at his notes. "'Sexless in the City,'" he starts. Then, he raises his eyes to Jarrod. "I noticed you do a lot of segments about the best places to meet someone or how to create the most compelling Internet dating profile. You even had a few 'Best Sex' segments in the last few weeks on how to increase libido. I thought we could do something about the young twenty- and thirty-somethings in the city who are still virgins. Look at why they're making the choices they are and follow them on a night out on the town. It has to be difficult, having that conversation with a potential hook-up."

Jarrod's head is bobbing in interest at this idea.

"It's lame," I say.

The room turns to me.

I look to Jarrod. "No one cares about a bunch of Bible Belt virgins saving themselves for marriage."

Everyone in the room looks down at their notes on the table, afraid to argue with the great and powerful Heather.

Except for one person.

Of course.

"It doesn't have to be for religious reasons. Maybe they just value their bodies," Ryan defends. "And so what if it is about religion? We should shun them because they're not spreading their legs for everyone?" He leans in, his words directed toward me. "Or is that what you're supposed to do in your twenties? Screw everything that moves."

I purse my lips. "So, you think women who go out and have one-night stands are whores?"

"I never said that."

"You said they don't value their bodies."

"I said, there is something admirable about a person who wants to wait to share themselves with the one special person they plan to share their life with."

"So, following a stranger up to their apartment would make that person a disgrace?" I turn to Jarrod. "I think we should explore the art of the one-night stand. We'll call it, 'Sleeping with a Stranger,' exploring what compels a person to go home with someone they don't know."

"That's an interesting—" Jarrod starts.

"Go home with a stranger? What would compel a person to ask a stranger into their home in the first place? In today's day and age, it can be quite dangerous," Ryan barks from his side of the room.

"'City Slickers,' about con artists who leave out critical information about themselves in order to bed women," I counter.

"'City Suckers,' women who only date men with power," Ryan nearly shouts.

"Men who make women feel bad about the choices they make." I rise from my chair, my hands splayed on the table.

"Women who marry for money," Ryan sneers.

That last line gets Jarrod's attention, who turns and looks down at my hand with a slight rise of his brows. He quirks a grin. "Well, it looks like we have our own War of the Roses thing in here."

The room chuckles at his comment. I take a seat and adjust my hair. I haven't gotten that worked up in a meeting in years.

Jarrod looks to me. "I think you and Ryan make a good team. Take him under your wing." To Ryan, he says, "You're getting a first-class education in production, working with Heather. Consider this a gift. I think you two will come up with some interesting story ideas."

My jaw drops, and I'm about to protest when Jarrod rises and speaks in a louder than usual voice, "I have an announcement to make."

Please don't. Please don't. Please don't.

"Heather and I are getting married." His words are matter-of-fact.

I rub my forehead with the pads of my fingers. There is silence as the staff processes what Jarrod just said. It isn't until Meg starts the awkward slow clap that everyone follows suit and offers their congratulations.

Jarrod leaves without acknowledging a single pat on the back or a handshake. That leaves me to accept the good wishes from a roomful of people who don't like me.

While I should care about their distaste for me, all I can think about is the man on the other side of the room who looks like he lost the war.

chapter FOUR

The problem with taking someone under your wing is, you have to guide them. That only works if you know the direction you want to go.

"Ryan, the intern, is in your office," Meg says as I round the corner, coming in from a morning meeting.

My Pradas halt on the carpet squares. "Why?"

"It's your one-on-one session." Her words are slow, explaining this as if it were common knowledge to everyone.

I force a look of disgust. "Reschedule for next week. I'll be down the hall. Come fetch me when he's gone."

"With all due respect, you *have* canceled on him. Three times." Meg looks at me over her red-framed glasses. "I know you don't usually mentor, but he's a really nice kid. Mr. Bellomy is your fiancé, but he's still your boss, and since he's assigned you to look after Ryan, I think you owe the boy at least fifteen minutes of your time."

My body is arched back. My eyebrows are hovering over my eyes. If I had a Q-tip, I'd clean my ears to make sure I'd just heard what I thought I did. "Where is Meg, and what have you done with her?"

Her mouth flies open, and a series of gasps follows. "I'm sorry, Heather. I don't usually meddle but—"

I hold up my hand to her. "No, I like it. Everyone around here is too nice. It's good to have a woman with some brass balls in the building."

Meg nods her head, her hands meekly crossed in front of her body.

With an exasperated breath, I walk into my office and pause at the broad shoulders of the man sitting in the chair opposite my desk. He's facing the windows, looking out to the river. His leg is resting on the opposite kneecap, his foot dancing in the air with nervous energy.

I stand in the doorway and look at the back of Ryan in a way I shouldn't. Like someone who knows what it's like to be held in those arms all night as he runs his finger up and down her arm while he tells stories of growing up in Chicago. Like someone who wants to sit on his lap and play with the curls at the end of his hair, asking him to tell her more jokes. Like someone who wants to rub her palms over his tensely held shoulders to take away the stress and work out the knots and kinks. Maybe do a goofy impression and see that incredible grin of his again. No other employee in this building would cause me to stop and stare the way I am right now even if it's only at the back of his head.

Suddenly, his foot stops shaking. His shoulders rise with a deep inhale, his head lifting with the movement.

Ryan addresses me without turning his head, "Are you coming in, or are you just going to stare at me all day?"

I startle at the accusation.

Pushing my shoulders back, I walk into the room and take a seat at my desk. I turn to the screen of my computer and start scrolling with my mouse, moving it around the desktop, even though I have nothing worthy of looking up at the moment. Still, it's better than facing him.

I open an email to Meg and start typing.

With my eyes on the screen, I flatly say to Ryan, "What can I do for you?"

His body is stiff, controlled. There is no movement coming from him. Just the deep bass of his voice. "Surprised you showed."

I answer, unimpressed, "You get ten minutes. Give me your three best story ideas."

"I'll wait until you're done typing. You seem distracted."

My fingers pause on the keyboard, my eyes still on the computer screen. "I have to get this memo out. It's far more intriguing than 'Sexless in the City.'" I throw in an annoyed sigh for good measure.

"Actually, I was thinking of another story line. Something a bit more human interest," he says.

My curiosity is piqued.

God, if I could only just give myself the opportunity to look at him, I'd bet he had that sideways smirk on his face. Or maybe he's biting his lip, the way he does with the side of his mouth pulled in, making the rest jut out in a way that makes me want to suck on it.

I swallow hard and take a deep breath, cleansing myself of the ridiculous thought, before I start typing again. "And?"

"It's called 'Never Have I Ever.' We take the anchors and all the correspondents, even the weather girl, and find out what they've always wanted to do but never have, and then we follow them on that experience."

"Been there, done that." In my defense, I'd be this rude to any staff member. I consider myself an equal-opportunity bitch.

He doesn't seem to notice. "Not on this show and not like this. It would run once a week for five weeks, and after that, we'd have viewers write in with something they'd never done. The traffic it would drive to our social media pages would be insane. We could even use Facebook Live and record the events as we were filming them. Make it interactive, as if the show were going on beyond the broadcast time."

And, now, my fingers halt completely.

That's actually a really good idea.

My eyes are fixated on the letter *G* on the keyboard as I decide if I should be mean and run Ryan out of my office or take the high road and address him like the adult he is.

I swallow my pride, hit Send on the email I was typing to Meg, and turn to Ryan. He's looking at me. His masculine jaw is jutted out, and the perfect arch of his brow is curved in as he waits for a response.

I place my hands on my lap and rub them on the chiffon fabric of my dress. "What kind of experiences do you have in mind?"

Ryan's chin relaxes, and his cheekbones rise as he looks down at his paper and reads his notes. "I spoke to our anchors, and Chad said he always wanted to go skydiving."

I roll my eyes. How many times has someone filmed their first time skydiving? Though I wouldn't mind pushing Misty Waters out of a plane…sans parachute.

"But," Ryan says, "I told him that was cliché, so we worked on other ideas. After some digging, I learned that our boy Chad has always wanted to tap dance."

I must have a look of confusion on my face because Chad Lyons is this burly ex-football player who became a television host after his retirement from the NFL. Apparently, the television industry has become a place for people who can no longer play sports. Go figure.

Ryan continues, "'Never Have I Ever Tap-Danced.' I know it doesn't sound that great, but trust me when I tell you, anyone who watches football would go crazy over seeing Chad dance. It would be all over the Internet."

I sway my head from side to side. "I'm not crazy about it, but I like where the idea is headed." Despite myself, I lean forward and say, "You're looking at producing a series, which is very ambitious, but you have to look at the business side. How is this going to move the show forward, toward the greater goal?"

"Ratings?"

"Revenue." I pick up a pen and write down some notes. "We could team up with Broadway in Chicago and have them sponsor the series. I'll find out what shows they have that need a boost in sales and have them cast Chad in one for a performance."

Ryan nods. "That's a great idea."

"It was yours. Now, you have to find more experiences to make this worthy of a five-week series for February sweeps. That gives us enough time to pre-produce all the moving parts."

"That's five months away."

"Good things come to those who plan early."

I laugh lightly with my comment, but when I look up, I see Ryan's face is far from laughing. He's looking at me seriously. The look makes my body still and my heart race.

"Sometimes, the very best things show up unannounced."

His words hit my heart in a place that has been thickly coated with a force field that protects it from feeling the way it is right now because I know exactly what he means. I hadn't planned on meeting Ryan, but he happened anyway.

"Do you have a Never Have I Ever?" he asks.

I blink. "Me? No. I've done just about everything I've ever wanted."

"Not even something mediocre? Something you have always wanted to try but never have?"

I look down and think of something I've never done. My thoughts immediately go to the time I begged my parents to take me to a local carnival. We couldn't go because we didn't have the money. Imagine that? A two-dollar ticket was more than we could afford.

It's a simple experience that was lost on me. It's childish, so I've never talked about it. Until now.

"I've never been to a fair. You know, ridden a Ferris wheel or a roller coaster. I've never even been on a carousel." I wave my hand in the air in a blasé way.

"Every girl deserves a ride on a carousel." His words are sincere, and the way his eyes glisten as he says them makes my heart melt. "Heather," Ryan says my name, the low-pitch sound of his voice like a whisper in the air.

I look over at him and am struck with just how handsome he is—the masculine line of his jaw, the perfectly formed nose, and the intense deep-set eyes and thick lashes. Those thick lashes fall on my ring. His face hardens, and I pull my hand back onto my lap.

"Excuse me," Meg says as she knocks on my door.

I look up and see her standing with a printed piece of paper in her hand.

I raise my brows to her, asking what she needs.

53

Meg looks to Ryan and then to me. "Sorry if I'm interrupting, but"—she holds the paper up in the air—"why did you send me the lyrics to 'Amazing Grace'?"

My head falls to my hand in mortification. I mean, what else do you type when you're pretending to be busy? Clearly, the answer is "Amazing Grace."

I roughly wipe my brow in a move that's half-embarrassment, half-annoyance. "We'll discuss it after my meeting."

I shoo her away as best as I can, and when she is out of earshot, I look at Ryan, who is staring me down with a gaze so fierce, I fear I might fall apart in my chair. My breath hitches, and I have to put my facade back on or else he'll completely tear down my walls.

With a clearing of my throat, I settle back into position and resume typing on my computer. "It's time you go back to work. I want the additional experiences in my mailbox tomorrow." I lick my lips and purse them tightly. "I think you should start meeting with one of our producers who will guide you through the process."

"I thought you were gonna be my mentor?" he asks.

I answer him by breathing in through my nose as I pull up the website for a high-end wedding dress designer, and then I start scrolling through her collection.

He sits for a moment, clearly not in a rush to get up. I can feel his stare shooting into me like a laser beam, but I pretend to ignore it. I lift my chin and continue to scroll and click. He must get bored of watching me because he rises from his seat. As he walks to the door, I sneak a glance and am suddenly reminded of how impressive his physique is.

In my head, I keep telling myself that he's just a boy. But, in reality, he's all man.

Ryan walks to the door, and just as he's about to walk away, he turns and says, "Are you the wretch who needs to be saved?"

My body freezes. I won't turn to him, but the question is enough to make me lose all conscious thought.

"Is that what you think of me? I'm a wretch?" I ask.

He shakes his head. "No, Heather, I think you're lost. You just need to be found."

"There you are, love!"

Jarrod is seated at his usual table at La Riviere. I walk over to him for our lunch date, place a kiss on his cheek, and take a seat. I'm laying a white linen napkin on my lap when a waiter appears.

"Tito's, on the rocks," I say to the waiter, earning me a grimace from my fiancé.

"Imbibing so early in the day?"

"It's after noon. Besides, I'm having an off day."

"Busy morning?"

"Just a meeting with the intern."

"Ah, Ryan Pierson. Good-looking young man. I'm sure he has his pick of women, don't you think?"

I turn back to the waiter. "Make it a double."

The waiter leaves, and I fix my napkin again. It just won't stay flat on my lap.

"He has a face for television. We should groom him before he gets a job somewhere else. Maybe put him on the program, perhaps as a model or something. See how he does."

I play with the napkin again, finally getting it to settle on my thighs.

"Is everything all right?" Jarrod asks.

My head shoots up. "Yes, sorry. Distracted." I lay my hand across the table and take Jarrod's in mine.

He thumbs the ring on my finger. "Looks stunning on you. Nothing but the best for the future Mrs. Bellomy."

I smile at the sight of my ring. It is exquisite. "Everything I have ever wanted." *Isn't it?*

The waiter reappears with my vodka and offers me a menu.

Jarrod holds up a hand. "No need. We know what we want. I'll have the poached wild salmon steaks with citrus beurre blanc, and she'll have the shaved asparagus salad, hold the Gouda and the hazelnuts."

As the waiter walks away from the table, I eye Jarrod, wondering why he would order my favorite salad but tell the waiter to remove the best parts.

He answers without me asking, "We don't want you fattening up like a little piggy, do we?"

My jaw falls open. "I didn't realize my weight was a concern."

"It's not," he says with a cavalier smile. "And we want to keep it that way."

I lift my glass to my mouth and take a sip—a long, indulging sip. When I'm done, I offer him a closed mouth smile and then say, "No, we wouldn't want that."

"Isn't that just a wretched thought?" he says, causing me to flash my doe eyes at him.

"Excuse me?"

"You. Fat. Can you imagine?" His voice is in disbelief of the notion.

Good thing he didn't see me in high school. Acne, glasses, braces…I was quite the sight.

I'd like to say I was marrying a man who would love me no matter what I looked like, but that's not the case. I didn't choose that sort of man to marry. I handpicked this one because he is more superficial than I am.

If I wanted to marry someone who'd love me no matter what, I'd be with someone like…never mind.

I can't afford to think that way.

Well, after I marry Jarrod, I'll be able to afford anything I want.

"Heather, is that who I think it is?" he asks, causing me to turn my head.

"Who?"

Jarrod points a finger. "Over there. Alexander Asher. You used to work for him, no?"

Like whiplash, my head flies to the other side, my eyes roaming until I see the blond hair and golden eyes of the man I used to lust after. Not only is he attractive, but he also has more money than God. Like Jarrod, he's kind of an asshole, but I can deal with that. Obviously.

"Go say hello," he demands.

"No," I practically hiss at him.

"I'm surprised you didn't try to bed him, what with his empire and all," Jarrod says, which causes me to blush. "Oh, I see. You did try to bed the head of Asher Industries. Wise girl but not wise enough."

I lean back and feign insult. "Why do you say that?"

"Because he didn't want to marry for convenience. He married for love."

That is the most ridiculous thing I have ever heard. The Asher I knew used women just as much as they used him. While he could be fun at times, you couldn't get too close. He'd turn callous, vindictive. Hell, he even had a thing for married women because they wouldn't expect much from him in the form of commitment.

Still, I tried to turn him around, but he was like ice. A wall so sturdy, I couldn't penetrate it.

All for the best though because, now, I have Jarrod.

"And you know this how?" I fold my arms in front of my body and raise my brows.

Jarrod speaks as if he is saying the most disgusting thing in the world, "He gave up his claim to his billion-dollar inheritance."

My face scrunches up in confusion. "Are you telling me the man is broke?" I look back at Asher. He is decked out from head to toe in a designer suit and shoes and a twenty-thousand-dollar Rolex. "He hardly looks like he is struggling for cash."

"It's true. Now, imagine if you'd married him and the next day he told you he was walking away from all that money?" He tsks and continues, "Don't worry. I promise you, I will never walk away from my trust." He gives me a wink and takes a sip of his Pellegrino.

I turn back to Asher. He's seated at a table, looking down at his iPhone. With his lush lips, square jaw, and perfectly tanned skin, he looks like a god among mortals. His face is stern as he reads whatever it is on his screen, but something catches his attention, and he looks up. Whatever it is makes his eyes dance and his cheeks rise.

A blonde woman walks to the table. She is pretty but not overly beautiful. She has dark eyes and a heart-shaped face. Asher rises from his table and greets the woman with a kiss. But not just any kiss. He places his hands on the sides of her face and pulls her in with an embrace so intimate, I feel like I'm interrupting their sacred moment just by being in the same room.

When he pulls back, she looks up at him like the world is in his eyes. And he is looking back at her the same way.

The two take a seat and start talking and laughing. She has a gorgeous ring on her finger, and he has a simple band. This is not some taken woman he is shacking up with for the weekend. The bond between them is clear. This is his wife.

An odd thought strikes me.

Some people really do marry for love. Well, it seems Asher married for love. The verdict is still out on Miss Thang over there.

I turn to Jarrod. "Why would he give up his inheritance?"

He is looking at his iPhone, probably answering emails. He talks while typing, "No one knows. Now, he's doing something with music. I can't quite remember. Nevertheless, he's married, and I give it six years before she finds someone whose pockets are lined deeper than his."

I let out an amused snort. "I give them six months."

"In for the night?" Charlie, my doorman, asks as I walk into the lobby of my building.

"Yes." I walk over to his desk. "Any deliveries?"

Charlie looks under his desk and pulls out a UPS envelope. "This came for you."

He hands it over, and I look at the sender—Joseph Vance, Private Investigator.

I take it and don't miss the questioning look Charlie is giving me.

He leans down, grabs something out from the space beneath him, and lifts it up. In his hand is a pair of boring brown shoes. "I also have these." Charlie is holding up Ryan's shoes from that fateful night. "He was awfully chipper when he came through here. Asked where there was a nearby coffee shop."

A smile tugs on my lips, but I pull it back. "Surprised you let him back up without my permission. I could have been dead."

"I am a doorman, not a security guard. You want to bring random men into the building? That is your prerogative." He nods to the shoes. "My only requirement is that I do not return *these*."

I blow a stray piece of hair off my face. "You can toss them."

I start to walk toward the elevator, leaving Ryan's shoes with Charlie. I'm not walking into my office and handing Ryan his shoes, only to have someone notice. He can buy a new pair.

"Wait." I turn around and walk back to Charlie. "I'll take them." I hold out a hand.

He hands me the size eleven shoes. "Change of heart?" His white brows are furrowed over his eyes.

I squint at the old man. "The kid doesn't have a paying job. Maybe I'll ship them to him or something."

Charlie makes a harrumph sound. "As you wish…"

"What?" I ask with a tapping foot.

"Nothing, nothing," His mouth is downturned as he starts fiddling with papers and whatnot on his desk. "You seemed rather pleasant the next day."

As in, I'm not pleasant every other day? "He's only twenty-one."

This causes Charlie to laugh. "When I was his age, I had two kids and had fought in a war."

My parents had me before they were old enough to drink, and look at where that led them. People under a certain age shouldn't make life decisions.

"How did that turn out for you?" I ask with rudeness to my tone.

"Thirty years later, and she's still the most beautiful woman I've ever laid eyes on," he says with metaphorical stars in his eyes.

"You're one of the rarities then." I slide my purse further up my shoulder. My ring catches the light and Charlie's attention.

"I take it, he wasn't the one to give you that piece of jewelry. Do I know the lucky fellow?"

"Yes. Jarrod. Dark skin. Salt-and-pepper hair—"

"Comes late at night and leaves before the sun comes up," he says.

"Charlie!" While I'm quite fond of my doorman, I'm learning that he certainly is the old washwoman.

"Just an observation." He tilts his head. "Besides, you're a smart, successful woman, living in a place like this. You know what's best."

I slowly nod my head and turn away from him. I've made the right decisions for thirty-one years. I'm not about to start questioning myself when I'm so close to my goal.

"I hope you find who you're looking for," he says, forcing me to turn around.

When I do, I see he's eyeing up the envelope in my hand.

"How did you know I was looking for someone?"

He leans in, and his pale eyes soften. "Heather, you're the only person in this building who doesn't have family come to visit."

Observant people. Watch what you say around them and what you *don't* say around them.

"And to think, I once called you charming."

I hit the elevator button and step into the car. When it arrives on my floor, I walk to my apartment, open the door, and kick off my shoes.

I have yoga pants on and a glass of vodka in my hand in no time.

I'm standing in my kitchen, the UPS mailer on the counter. It's the contract for the investigator I hired to find my dad. I don't know why I'm even doing this. The man can rot on the streets for all I care. He's a despicable human being who treats women like shit.

Especially his daughter.

"I got you a job. Dancing," he said one night, drunk off his ass.

His wifebeater was riding up, causing his gut to appear between his shirt and his jeans. His denim button-down was open and hanging around his bulging stomach.

I was only fifteen, but I knew exactly what kind of dancing he was referring to. "Dancing where?"

"Pinkies in Astoria." He had a look of pride on his face.

My history book was lying in front of me as I tried to study, so I could actually go to college and not be a stripper at the club where his current girlfriend danced.

"I'm underage," I said with disgust.

He waved me off and started walking toward his room. "They all are."

"You're a pig," I called after him.

"And you're useless." He slammed the door behind him.

I push the contract in the trash and walk into my living room. A barren room, void of any reference to life or family. It's just filled with *things*.

I fall to my knees and open the bottom door of the entertainment unit. Inside is a bronze box, ornate in detail, with rose filigree. I open it and take out the only personal artifacts of my childhood.

At the top is a newborn hospital hat. It has a smear of dried blood on it, obviously the one I wore the day I was born. I hold it in my hands and feel the soft fabric between my fingers. It used to smell like baby powder. Now, it just smells stale, like it's been trapped in a box for three decades.

Next, I take out a tiny pink bear with the words *Mommy's Little Cub* written on the belly. I'd like to think she loved me once upon a time in order to have kept these things. I've thought about hiring someone to find her, but I never will. She left me. She might not have wanted *him*, but she deserted her only child.

I push past a few knickknacks—most from school, like a medal for winning the science fair and an eraser set given to me by the first boy I ever had a crush on. I don't know why I still have it, but I do.

At the bottom of the box is a picture. It's faded, and it has my fingerprints indented on it. In the photo is a man. He has shaggy dark hair that falls around his ears and a mustache that rounds down to his chin. He looks like he's sleeping, but he's not. His eyes are closed in a peaceful moment, a smile on his lips. In his arms is a sleeping baby, snuggled close to his chest, content and safe in her father's embrace.

It's a picture of me and my dad.

I don't know what happened or why he changed. It doesn't matter. All I know is that, for one fleeting moment, a moment long enough for someone to grab a camera and take a picture, he loved me.

I'm sure my parents had no idea when they named me, but heather is a plant that thrives in decaying lands. That's me. Thriving in a home that slowly fell apart each year until there was nothing left but sadness and pain.

I place everything back in the box and close the door. With my back against the wall, I bring my knees to my chest and stare at the carpet. The same carpet I danced on with a beautiful man, feeling right for the first time in my life.

A man who, despite only knowing him for one night, has captured my soul and made it flourish in his light.

A man who I wish I would stop dreaming about.

A man who I secretly wish I could be with.

A man who I need to stay far away from.

chapter FIVE

It's been four weeks since Ryan started his internship, which also means it's been four weeks of enduring certain office chatter.

"What are they feeding these boys these days?"

"They didn't look like that when I was in college."

"Forget compliance. I'd risk my job for one night with that."

The chitchat of the office girls in the break room makes me over pour the milk into my tea.

"Damn it," I mutter as I use a napkin to brush away the milk dribbling down my skirt.

"You okay there, Heather?" Michaela, a sexy New Zealander with dark skin and a too-friendly smile, cautiously asks me.

It's not like anyone on the staff to talk to me about anything other than their assignments.

"I'm fine." I toss the napkin in the trash and adjust my skirt.

When I look up, three girls are staring at me.

"So, when's the wedding?" Michaela asks.

The other girls are now staring into their coffee cups.

As much as I don't want to like her, the truth is, she's really nice. Like, annoyingly sincere in a way that seems fake but you know it is genuine.

"We haven't set a date," I answer. Then, I grab my tea off the counter to leave.

"You make a beautiful couple," Michaela says.

I wonder if she chose the word *beautiful* over *wonderful* or *happy* or even *loving* for a reason.

Because we're not. Any of those things.

"Thank you," I say. I leave the room before any more questions are asked. I'm not two feet outside the door when I hear the other two bitches snickering from the break room.

Who cares? I got the guy. And the funds. They're just jealous.

I walk my tea toward my office but pause when I see Ryan chatting with Zahara, one of the other interns, in the hallway. Ducking inside an office, I take cover so as not to be seen.

I've been doing this a lot lately.

It sucks, having to see him everywhere. Since Jarrod put Ryan under my wing, and our failed one-on-one mentoring session, we keep our conversations strictly business and low on eye contact. It's an arrangement we made in silence.

Yet, every once in a while, I catch him looking, and I pretend my heart isn't beating out of my chest at the sight. Like when I'm in the control room, microphone set on my head, calling out orders to the director and telling the tech guys when to get the graphics on-screen, I'm in the moment, trying to keep our live broadcast on schedule, looking as clean as possible...and then I see him.

Ryan.

He's just standing in the corner, watching me like he's never seen someone produce a television show, never seen a woman man the helm of a broadcast and dictate orders to others. The look on his face is not one of intimidation. It's admiration. And it kills me.

Or, the other day, when the whole show imploded. Guests canceled, props went missing, and our host started freaking out because someone took her weave from the dressing room. I was scrambling like a chicken with its head cut off, and when I got to my office, there was a grande chai tea waiting for me. I asked Meg if she left it. She said no and wasn't sure who had. I'm pretty sure I knew though.

You know what kills me the most? He's smart. Over the past few weeks, I've had the honor of sitting in on various meetings where he brings up the latest trends in news. He has an uncanny way of knowing what is going to be on everyone's mind the next day.

And he's kind. I witnessed him giving a homeless guy twenty bucks. That has to be a lot on a college student's salary, especially one who is working an unpaid internship.

He's the type of guy who comes in early and stays late just to help other people get their work done.

And, Lord help me, when he volunteered to be a model in our "Summer Splash Swimsuit" demo on the show, the baby-soft skin of a young twenty-one-year-old over the rippling muscles of a former football player brought back memories that are still too fresh in my mind to easily recover from.

"Not only am I going to lick your sweet pussy until you're screaming my name, I am also going to fuck you until the sun comes up."

"Can I help you with something?" Michaela appears next to me in the hallway.

I jolt back with my hand over my heart.

"No." I pause. "I was just waiting for someone. I have a meeting." I awkwardly point to the office I am half-standing, half-hiding in.

Michaela's dark eyes dart to the space behind me. A desk and an empty chair are in the room. "That's my office," she states in that Kiwi accent.

"Oh." I step into the hall. "My bad, I thought this was—" I can't make up anything on the fly, especially because, when I look to my right, Ryan and Zahara are looking my way. I pivot to the left and smack into Meg, who is walking down the hall.

Hot.

Burning hot.

Steam.

"I'm so sorry, Heather. Did you burn yourself?" Meg asks, fanning down my chest with rapid hand movements where my cup of tea just crashed into me.

My skin is on fire. I pick up the lapel of my shirt and start pumping it away from my chest, a poor attempt at creating a breeze. Making quick work of my feet, I scurry down to the break room, which, thankfully, is empty, and I turn on the sink faucet to splash cold water on my chest.

My blouse is soaked. My skirt now has milk and tea stains, and I, quite possibly, have second-degree burns on my skin. All in all, I'd say this is a *fabulous* day.

The door behind me opens. I close my eyes in mortification of who in the world could be in here. I think the only person I can tolerate right now is Meg, but she knows better than to bother me. I'm sure whoever it is loves the front-row view of my embarrassment.

The body behind me walks around to the refrigerator.

It doesn't take long for the tall, well-built frame and perfectly defined ass in a pair of Dockers to make its way into my peripheral vision, sending my body into a frenzy. I can pick Ryan out of a lineup of a thousand men—blindfolded. There's just something about his presence, his aura, that appeals to my senses.

He opens the freezer door and takes out a tray of ice cubes, pouring them into a Ziploc bag. He turns to me and pauses. That scowl from the last few times he's looked at me is gone. Slowly, he walks toward me, stopping just a few feet away.

"May I?" he asks, holding the bag up in the air.

I nod and let out a sigh of defeat.

He closes the gap, the heat of his body hotter than the tea on my skin. He's wearing his glasses, and they make him look so much older and sexier than his twenty-one years.

He lifts the bag to my chest, and I insert a hiss at the cold feeling against my heated skin. It stings at first, but then I let out a light moan when relief quickly sets in.

"I see I was right," he says.

"About what?"

"You like tea." His mouth is quirked to the side.

Memories of the sweet note and that beautiful rose that has since died and disposed of in the trash come back to me.

I was happy. Genuinely happy. The euphoric feeling is gone, and I seem to get glimpses of it every time he's in the room.

I fight a grin. "I love tea. And bagels."

Ryan moves the ice around my chest. Each move stings but is followed by comfort.

"You have a beautiful smile, Heather. You don't smile enough."

His gaze focuses on mine, and I can see my smile in the reflection of his glasses.

"I don't have many things to smile about," I say truthfully.

His face falls, but those eyes stay tuned in on me. "I don't know about that. Aren't newly engaged women usually the happiest they've ever been?" He takes my hand with his free one and raises it to my chest, placing it over the ice. When my hand is secure, he removes his and steps back. "You got what you want. You should be happy."

"I am," I say with a cough. "I'm really excited. Jarrod and I have been planning the big day. He'll make an amazing husband."

Ryan nods. His hands go in his pockets as he retreats back a step. "Good, because that would be a sin to spend eternity with someone who doesn't make you happy."

I swallow, trying to find words, something to say.

"She used to dance." My eyes are trained on a white button on his shirt. "My mother. When I was little, we always had music in the house. She would put on these little shows. I didn't realize it at the time, but she was probably drunk. Still, those moments, they were the best memories." I inhale a shaky breath. "I haven't danced with anyone since she left. The thought of being held by someone else when she didn't want to do so hurt too much. I've avoided it for too long."

His chin nods as he takes in the severity of what I just said.

I look up into his eyes, the ones I've feared staring into, knowing I'd lose myself completely.

JEANNINE COLETTE

I continue, "That night...our night, when you danced with me...it meant more than you could ever imagine." I don't know why I'm telling him this. It just feels like something I'm supposed to do.

Ryan lifts a hand and tucks my hair behind my ear. With his thumb, he wipes a stray tear I didn't know I'd shed. I nod into his hand, savoring the feeling.

"Thank you for telling me." He rubs a small circle on my cheek. "Heather, that night, with you, it was the most—"

His words are cut off when the door to the break room opens. Meg peeks her head in, her eyes bugging out for a second, and then she retreats backward for a moment. Something in her eyes changes as she takes in the sight of Ryan with his hands on me, the intimate embrace we are sharing. She moves back into the room and stands there, looking at us like a mother hen getting her chickens in line.

Ryan's body stiffens. When he releases me, I feel so alone.

I watch as Ryan walks to the break room door and nods to Meg. A secret conversation passes between them.

He turns around to me and says, "Take care of yourself." He points to my burn, but I have a feeling this is his way of giving up on us.

On our one night.

On our standoff.

On our coexistence.

The door closes behind him. I lean my hip against the counter, the ice on my heart and my hand on my head.

"He's an intern." Meg's words pull me out of my sorrow.

I lift my head to her. "Excuse me?"

"You're senior level management and, not to mention, Jarrod Bellomy's fiancée. He's a student. It's against company policy to fraternize with the interns. It's also tabloid fodder to be caught in an intimate embrace with a boy who is still in school."

"It wasn't—" I stop, trying to find the words. "What you saw, that was just..."

Meg frowns her lips, unhappy with me. Unhappy with what she saw. Unhappy with this role reversal the two of us seem to be sharing.

"Unless you want to destroy that boy's good name and your own, you'd better stay away from him."

Meg leaves the room, and I fall further into myself. My eyes are heavy, and before I know it, tears start trickling down my face. I haven't cried since I was a kid, and here I am, in the goddamn break room, sobbing like a baby.

Perhaps tears are a side effect of getting burned.

chapter SIX

Seven p.m., and every soul in the building is rushing out to get home after a long day's work. The sound of people flocking through the lobby to get home drowns out the sound of my four-inch Pradas as I walk through the lobby. I swing through the revolving door onto Wacker Drive and raise my arm to hail a cab.

The yellow taxi reminds me of New York as it pulls up in front of me. I step off the curb. As soon as my fingers hit the handle, another hand is on top of mine.

"Well, this is some coincidence," I say as I take in the male standing against me. I don't even have to look up to know it is Ryan.

"Who said it was a coincidence?"

That voice makes my heart beat fast. If I could cover my ears, I would.

"What are you doing, Ryan?" I open the door and step inside the open frame, Ryan standing on the other side of the door.

"Where are you going?" he asks.

"Dinner with Jarrod." I lower my shoulders and get into the cab.

He holds the door open. "Someplace fancy?"

Shrugging my shoulders, I reach over to the door, preparing to close it. "Sushi."

Ryan places his body in between me and the open door, halting me from closing it. He bends his body, so he's looking into the cab. "You hate sushi."

He's correct. "What's your point?"

The cab driver turns around. "I don't have all day, guys."

If we keep this up, Ryan and I will have our photos placed in every taxi depot in the city with a note that reads, *Do not pick up this fare. They won't let you leave the curb.*

"Run the meter," Ryan commands. He watches as the driver does so. Then, he turns back to me and says, "Come with me."

I look down at my tea-stained shirt and my milky skirt. "I don't have time for this. I still have to go home and change and meet Jarrod—"

"Cancel." His stance is stern, powerful.

His words force me to look up at him, and I'm damned for doing so. His cobalt blues are staring at me in earnest. He is a man set on a mission and won't back down until he gets what he wants. What he needs.

"Why would I do that?" I ask, afraid of how he might answer. Afraid of how my heart will react.

"Because you want to," he says. "Take a chance on me. Just for tonight. One last time, and then I swear, you will never have to see me again. You'll marry one of the wealthiest bachelors in Chicago and live happily ever after. But at least you'll know that, for one night, just once, you had a great time with a guy who only has eighty bucks in his pocket, fulfilling his dream of taking a beautiful girl dancing in Chicago."

My heart stops beating at the sound of the most incredible proposal I've ever heard.

When I don't immediately answer, Ryan adds, "Besides, you think I have a great personality."

I fall back in the seat and raise a brow. "When did I ever say you had a great personality?"

"It's known. That, and the fact that I have a great ass. I've seen you checking it out." He flashes that award-winning Midwestern smile. "Despite what you think, I'm a sought-after bachelor myself. In ten years, you are going to be kicking yourself if you don't let me take you out just one last time."

"I will, will I?"

"Yep," he says. He scoots me over in the seat. He doesn't even give me a chance to say yes before he closes the door.

I can't believe he is hijacking my evening.

"I can't go anywhere like this." I point to my ensemble.

Ryan looks down at my blouse and skirt, clearly noticing my disaster of an outfit for the first time. "You look perfect," he says in a sweet, seductive tone. "But, if it makes you feel better, then you can change." He turns to the driver and says, "LSD."

I raise a brow. Ryan laughs.

"Lake Shore Drive," he says. "We'll make a Chicagoan out of you soon enough."

Just like that, I am canceling my plans and going out for one last hurrah with Ryan Pierson.

We take a train into a working-class neighborhood that is a far cry from the bright lights and big buildings of Chicago. Ranch homes, close together, some with shared driveways, line the streets. A city park with a baseball field is at the nearest intersection.

"Where are we?" I ask, looking around at the kids playing ball in the street.

The sun is still bright, as it is in the summer evenings, making me happy I changed into shorts and sandals.

Ryan waited outside my building while I got dressed. When he saw the orchid-colored high-waist pleated shorts that look like a skirt and the matching tank I slipped on— paired together, they look like a dress—his face lit up all too appreciatively.

We turn a corner. Lush trees of green line the streets, stretching to the other side and connecting to one another like lovers.

"Since you got to change, so do I." He stops in front of a modest house with blue siding and a white door.

"This is your house?"

The front door is open, light laughter sounding from inside and somewhere in the back. A woman in the front window is talking to a young girl with long brown hair. Both have striking blue eyes.

"You live with your parents?" I didn't mean for my tone to sound so accusatory.

"Not everyone leaves home at sixteen. It's normal for people to live with their parents. At least, around here, it is."

There is a loud ruckus of cheering coming from the backyard. I tilt my body to see what is going on.

"That's my family," he answers my unasked question, walking up the stoop.

"Family?" I swallow with the question. My stomach drops, and my feet don't leave the cement walkway.

"Uncles, cousins—you know, family," he says. Then, he pauses. He turns around, his mouth parting as he inhales slightly with the realization.

Ryan walks back toward me, stopping just inches away. His hand rises and grazes my cheek. The feeling of warm skin on mine sends a lightning bolt of electricity down my spine.

"Hey," he speaks softly, "I'm just running in to change. If you don't feel comfortable, you can wait out here. Though I'd feel better if you came inside with me. You can wait in my room. Whatever you need."

His thumb runs a light circle on my skin. I look up into his handsome face and fall deep into the cobalt. His tender look consumes me, making me want to crawl into him like a warm security blanket. If he knew how his touch made me feel, how a single caress of his hand comforts me, how a hold while dancing makes me feel secure…

It feels like home.

The sound of a storm door closing breaks our moment.

We look over and see a man and a woman standing on the stoop, looking surprised. The man is tall, like Ryan, with a full head of dark hair and dimples to match his son's.

Ryan places a hand behind my back and escorts me to the couple who meet us on the sidewalk. The woman, who I presume is Ryan's mother, signs to Ryan.

He replies, "This is Heather McCallister. She is the senior producer." Then, he continues to sign something to her, which causes his mom to hit him in the arm with the wooden spoon she has in her hand.

I squeeze my lips together to keep from laughing.

"Hi," I say. Immediately, I feel stupid. They can't hear me. *Idiot.*

"Hello," his mother says.

My eyes dart up in surprise.

Ryan lets out a small laugh. His mother starts rapidly signing to him and motioning toward me.

Not wanting to get hit by his mother's hand or her spoon again, Ryan darts to the side, closer to me, and says, "Heather, these are my parents, Jenny and Fred Pierson."

I wave again, not saying anything.

"You can talk to them. I'll translate," he says.

"How do I know you won't change what I said and make something up?" I ask him.

"Because he knows his mother will kick his ass," his mom speaks and signs at the same time. Her words are spoken from the back of her throat. It's slightly difficult to understand but manageable.

I let out a laugh at her statement.

Ryan shakes his head with a smile. "Remember how I told you how hard it was growing up with deaf parents? They read lips. It's awful!"

His mother hits him with her spoon again, and I cover my mouth to contain my laughter.

His dad starts to sign, and Ryan translates, "*I don't know how you put up with my son. Smart-ass, this one.*"

"He's a hard worker. The brightest intern I've ever had on staff. You must be very proud," I say.

Ryan pauses in signing for a moment, seeming surprised by my compliment.

"*My son was supposed to go pro,*" Ryan translates what his mom signs. "*He was City Player of the Year in high school and First Team Conference Player of the Year at Northeastern.*"

I smile and nod to his mom, wondering if it bothers Ryan to have to talk for his parents, especially about himself.

"*Then, he hurt his foot, and his career ended. I'm happy he's found a new passion. I was never crazy about football. Always praying he wouldn't get hurt. But, now, he has a new path, and we are so thankful you have taken him under your wing. He says you are the smartest woman in television.*"

My head shoots toward Ryan, surprised he talks about me to his parents.

"Mom," Ryan says. Then, he starts signing to her without speaking his words.

His mom voraciously signs back while his dad curiously eyes me.

"Fine," he says. He turns back to me. "My mother would like me to invite you to stay at our house for dinner." Ryan says out of the side of his mouth, "I already told her we have plans. Besides, I'm trying to impress you, and a night with my family is not the answer."

His mother hits him in the arm again.

"Quit it, will you?"

Fred takes me by the arm and escorts me away from Ryan and his spoon-wielding mother. "Come, stay for one game," his father speaks, his speech less intelligible than Jenny's.

I follow the man down the driveway.

Ryan goes into the house to change, and I am brought into a backyard full of celebration with people talking and laughing. There's a long table in the center where a group is sitting down, playing a dice game. In the back is a barbecue with another table filled with food next to it.

Fred walks me over to a girl, about eighteen years old, with long brown hair and bright blue eyes, and he signs to her.

When he's done, she instantly shouts, "Ryan brought a girl home!"

78

Her words cause everyone in the backyard to stop what they're doing and look my way. I offer a pathetic wave.

She grabs my arm and pulls me into a hug.

"You must be Aubrie?" I guess, my arms hanging on the sides of her.

"I'm Andrea. Nice to know the lughead talks about us. Come, meet the family." She pulls me toward the big table.

"I'm not staying long. Just a few minutes."

The crowd has gone back to enjoying themselves.

I take in the tiki torches and lanterns decorating the backyard. "Is there a special occasion?"

Andrea shrugs. "No, this is just a typical Friday night," she says. Then, she stops for a second. "You're just as pretty as he said you were."

My face heats. I fear I'll turn bright red. "Ryan said I was pretty?"

Andrea's face lights up, her smile wide and bright. Then, she turns to the table of people playing a dice game. "This is Ryan's boss, Heather."

The group looks up.

"Supervisor," I correct.

An overweight man with a Jimmy Buffett shirt is the first to speak, "My supervisor doesn't look like you." He laughs as the woman next to him hits him in the side.

"Cut that out, Hal. Don't harass the girl," she says to him.

"What? My supervisor is a fat sack of—"

"All right, old man. Respect the lady," Andrea says. She pushes someone from the table and then ushers me toward the chair. "Sit here."

"No, I'm good."

"Please, sit," Fred says.

I find myself having a hard time saying no to him.

He signs to Andrea.

She looks down at me and asks, "Dad wants to know what you'd like to drink."

"Nothing for me. I'm not staying long!" I shout toward Fred. I feel like people are silently laughing at me.

Fred picks up a beer from the table. He points to it and then makes a thumbs-up. His head is bobbing, looking for a yes.

"Yes, that's perfect," I answer.

Andrea leans down and places a hand on my shoulder. With her other, she points to various people around the table. "Heather, these are our cousins—Nancy, Gia, Quinn, Mila, Amanda, and Brody. Uncle Hal and Aunt Maria. That's our neighbor Glen and my other uncle—John. Over there"—she points to the barbeque area—"are Uncles Bill and Tony and their wives, Sarah Jane and Leora. More cousins—Jack, Lucy, and Stacy. And my dad's friends from the Knights of Columbus—Gene, Frank, Mike K., and Mike P." She looks around the yard to see whom she's missing. "Oh, and that mess by the cooler are my friends Lisa and Anne."

"And this"—Hal holds up the three dice—"is Left Center Right. Have you ever played?"

I shake my head as he places three dollar bills in front of me.

"What's this for?" I ask.

"It's your ante. This is entirely a game of chance. You make no decisions of any kind. Just roll the die."

Hesitantly, I take the dice from him and roll them into the middle of the table. The letters L, R, and a dot appear on the dice.

"That's good," Andrea says, shaking my shoulders. "The L means you hand one of your dollars to the left, the R means you give one to the person to the right, and the dot means you keep one. As long as you have a dollar in front of you, you're in the game."

I hand one dollar to Nancy and another to John.

The dice get passed to Nancy, who rolls. She gets three dots. Everyone yells at the table that she fixed the roll.

"It's been a long time since Ryan brought a girl home," one of the cousins—I think her name is Mila—says.

"She's wearing a ring, moron," Quinn says as she rolls the dice. She gets R, R, and C.

The C means she has to put a dollar in the center. That dollar is now in the winner's pot and out of play for the rest of the game. Her other two dollars get passed to the right.

"Still, it's nice to see him bringing someone home, other than that whore, Maxine," Mila says as she takes her turn.

"They were on the fritz before everything happened," Aunt Maria says.

"Bullshit," Andrea utters from behind me. "She was just sticking around to see if he was gonna go pro."

Fred walks over and places a beer in front of me. I take a long swig of it and listen in on the conversation around me, getting whiplash from keeping up with the family banter.

"They dated for a year. That's a long time to devote to someone, only to have them dump your ass as soon as you get hurt," Hal says. Then, he hollers when he gets C, C, and R. "Goddamn it!"

The dice come around to John. He has to give me two dollars. I roll the dice and take my turn. Then, I pass the dice with three singles in front of me.

Jenny comes over and places a platter of chips and dip onto the table. The cousins start diving into the salsa. Jenny signs to Andrea.

She signs back to her mom as she says, "We were just talking about Maxine."

Jenny makes a pissed off face and then sticks her finger in her mouth, like she's gagging. The table laughs.

"*She was no good for Ryan,*" Andrea translates for her mom. "*They didn't have that connection. He'd walk into a room, and she wouldn't even look at him.*"

"Oh, hell, I haven't looked at Hal in years," Aunt Maria says with a laugh.

Hal pats himself on the gut. "Good thing. I've changed quite a bit over the last twenty-five years. Just keep on thinking of the guy you married on your wedding day."

Jenny shakes her head. "*When you are in love, especially young love, you're supposed to look at them like they are the only person in the room. When they speak, your heart races, and when they touch you—oh,*"

81

when you touch—it's like fireworks exploding on the Fourth of July,"
Andrea speaks for her mom.

I take a long drink of my beer. The cold bottle gives me
something to feel, other than the words Jenny just said. I
remember Ryan saying his parents were firm believers in love.
I've just never heard anyone speak of it so beautifully.

I clear my throat and play the game.

"I leave her for five minutes, and you wrangle her into a
game of LCR?" Ryan's soothing voice comes from the
background.

He pulls up a chair and sits behind me, maneuvering
himself slightly next to his Uncle John. He's changed into
blue cargo shorts and a beige crew neck T-shirt. His hair is
styled back in a loose yet perfect way. He smells like a fresh
shower.

When I look back toward the table, I see Jenny has a
knowing look in her eye, directed toward me. Her brows are
raised, and her mouth is quirked up.

"Looks like you're the ringer." Ryan motions to the
money in front of me and places a hand on my knee.

My current, the river inside me, flows with his touch.

"So, Heather, when is the wedding?" Aunt Maria asks.

Lost in the feeling of Ryan's hand on my skin, I have to
think about what she just asked me.

*Yes, the wedding. Why does everyone want to know the answer to
this question?*

"My fiancé hasn't picked a date yet."

Hal makes a cackling noise. "You're waiting for him to
pick a date? That's the girl's job. The groom just shows up."

I fake a smile. "We haven't gotten around to planning.
The engagement just happened. We're...settling into that.
Getting our paperwork in order."

"Paperwork?" Hal asks curiously.

Ryan saves me. "Heather is swamped with work. She's
brilliant at what she does."

I roll my eyes. "I don't think the staff would agree."

"That's who I heard it from," he says.

I twist around to face him.

"You're the best senior producer they've ever had. Before you came, the show was gonna be canceled. You saved it." He takes my beer off the table and starts drinking from it. "They're thankful for you. You just make it hard for them to show their appreciation."

I blink at Ryan a few times. Being *appreciated* by the staff is the last thing I expected.

"Your turn." John hands me the dice.

I roll them and get three dots. The table erupts in cheers and jeers.

We're toward the end of the game. Most of the dollars are piled in the center. Only a handful is floating around the table. We continue to pass the dice to whoever has bills in front of them, all while talking and joking. His family is fun and welcoming in a way I never expected. No one thinks it's odd that Ryan's engaged supervisor is here. No one questions why he is sitting so close to me or why he becomes overly excited when my chances of winning this silly game become greater.

This is what a family is like. What a home sounds like. It's warm, a place a person could easily become accustomed to remaining.

The game becomes intense. I even find myself getting enthusiastic about what other people's rolls are going to be. Dollars are passed left and right, and more are being placed into the center.

It comes down to me and Nancy. We each have a single dollar in front of us. If she gets a dot or an R, the game continues. If she gets a C or an L, the game is over, and I win.

Everyone starts banging on the table, like drummers. The movements make the table bounce.

Nancy blows on the dice, says a prayer to some saint, and then rolls them onto the middle of the table.

"L!" Ryan screams.

Everyone throws their hands up and yells.

"You won," he says, his hands on my shoulders, shaking me.

I won a grand total of thirty-three dollars, but they're applauding like I won the lottery.

When I look back at Ryan, his face is full of happiness. A simple happiness for my simple win. A huge smile breaks out on my face at the sight of him.

We decide to stay for another hour. I talk to some of Ryan's cousins, who are curious about the show we work on and how they can get into television, and Ryan's aunt, who wants to travel to New York and asked for restaurant recommendations. Every once in a while, I find myself looking over toward Ryan, who is playing with younger cousins or talking to a neighbor. Each time I look his way, he instinctually lifts his head and gives me a smile.

On a swing in the backyard, Jenny and Fred Pierson are sitting and swaying. Fred's arm is around Jenny. Her hands are holding both of his, one on her shoulder and the other on his lap. Her head is leaning into his shoulder as they look out onto the yard filled with friends and family. They're not talking. They are just two people sitting in complete silence, enjoying the warmth of each other's touch.

Jenny sees me watching her and Fred. She rises and walks over to where I'm standing. She gently asks the cousins to leave, but Maria stays behind.

"*I want to talk to you without my son watching. He's a nosy bastard*," Maria says for Jenny. Then, Maria adds on, "I agree."

I smile and then look toward Jenny as she uses her hands to form meaningful words.

"*I met Fred at school, here in Chicago. We were the only two deaf kids in a building of a thousand students. When we met, I wasn't hoping to fall in love. I just wanted a friend. And I got that from him. To be able to speak without outside influence, just listening to what the other is saying, you get to know a person more intimately than ever.*" She smiles, her eyes crinkling on the sides. "*Many people look at the deaf community as if we have a disability. But what they don't see is our ability to love deeper than imaginable. When Fred places his hand in mine, I feel his pulse racing through his veins. When he holds me, I can feel his breath on my skin in a way most people ignore. To love is not just to go through the motions. It's to feel every emotion. If you don't have that with the one you're with, then you're missing out on the greatest gift this life has to offer."*

A love as she describes, the way she has with her husband, sounds amazing. Beautiful. Unlike anything I've ever witnessed in my lifetime. A love I know I'll never feel.

"Thank you, Jenny. That was lovely. You are a lucky woman."

"Are you?" she asks, using her voice. "Does the man you love make you feel that way?"

The man I love? If she means Jarrod, then she has a different idea of the relationship we share.

"I was never looking for love," I answer honestly. "Where I come from, security is more important. What he offers me is exactly what I want."

Jenny's face falls, showing she is disappointed in my answer. "That is what you want. But is it what you need?"

I don't know what I need. I always thought, if I had financial security, I wouldn't need anything.

I look to Maria, who is waiting for my reply, but I don't have one. And, when I look over to the side, I see Ryan walking toward us, his eyes on mine. Without uttering a single word, we exchange a glance that says we're both ready to get out of here.

Suddenly, my needs and wants are becoming quite blurry.

chapter SEVEN

I've been escorted in Bentleys and private jets, taken to the most luxurious places in the world.

Right now, on the back of a Kawasaki Ninja, I am more at peace than I have been in my entire life.

Wearing one of Ryan's Northeastern sweatshirts and a helmet, I'm sitting high on the back of the bike, my body huddled around his. We are driving back toward the Chicago Loop. I dig my fingers into the seams of his shirt, my fingers tracing along the curve of his abs through the fabric. When we stop at a red light, he places a hand on my thigh and runs small circles on my soft skin.

We pull up in front of a restaurant. Ryan helps me off first and then follows.

"Pizza?"

He takes his helmet off and has an adorable case of helmet hair. "It was that or sushi," he teases.

I take off my helmet. My hair is probably sticking up in crazy directions, like his. I lean back and shake it out, like I'm in a Pantene commercial. Bringing my head back up, I'm rewarded with the Pierson grin I look forward to seeing.

I grab his hand and pull him toward the entrance. "Come on, show me what's so great about your *stuffed* pizza."

Giordano's pizza is like nothing I have experienced in Chicago. Laughter and cheers come from tables. Friends are dining, children are playing at the tables, and workers are bustling around, bringing pizzas and pitchers to tables. Each table is covered in a red-and-white-checkered tablecloth.

"What do you like on your pizza?" he asks as a waitress hands me a menu.

I shrug. "You pick. Isn't all pizza the same?"

I swear, the room goes silent.

Ryan just laughs. "She's from New York," he explains to the waitress, who is giving me the death stare. With a glorious smile, he says, "We'll have the Chicago Classic, one Sam Adams IPA and a…" He motions for me to order.

"The same," I say to her. Then, I turn to Ryan. "What's in the Chicago Classic?"

"Pepperoni, mushrooms, onions, and green peppers."

"In New York, the pizza's so good, all you need is cheese."

The waitress rips the menu from my hands, and I snicker as she walks away. *Man, these people take their pizza seriously.*

Ryan crosses his arms and leans his elbows on the table. "Tell me about New York."

So, I do. I tell him about the city that invented hip-hop and how I would sneak out of school early to go into Manhattan and stand outside *Total Request Live.* When Ryan says he's never heard of it, I don't make a joke about how much younger he is than me. I tell him about how it was the most amazing show on MTV, hosted by Carson Daly, where the best videos of the day were played and there was always a celebrity on set.

"Can you keep a secret?" I ask as I hold out my pinkie, making him swear never to tell a soul.

He wraps his pinkie around mine and seals it with a kiss. I might have let my pinkie linger around his mouth a moment too long.

"I was on a game show once. Well, not really a game show. It was called *Wanna Be a VJ.*"

His eyes widen in shock. "*Wanna Be a Vagina?*"

I kick him under the table. "No, *VJ*, as in video jockey. You compete to be the next MTV host."

"Did you win?"

"God, no. I was awful. I couldn't read the prompter. I paused when asked a question and stammered all over my words like an oaf. It was terrible." I recall the day I actually put myself out there and failed miserably. "God, I was nervous. That's why I went into production. I knew my days in front of the camera were long over."

He's sitting back in his seat, gazing sweetly at me. "I would have voted for you. With those big doe eyes and the sassiest mouth, you would have made an amazing VJ."

Well, damn if I'm not blushing.

Ryan tells me about his love for Chicago. From the Bears to the Bulls, he's a huge sports fan, but that's no surprise. His mom used to bundle him and his sisters up from head to toe in snow gear, and they looked like the kids from *A Christmas Story*. They would go swimming at his uncle's lake house in Michigan. And then he tells me the most disgusting recipe for a hot dog.

"All-beef dog on a poppy-seed bun, topped with tomato slices, white onions, relish, a pickle spear, peppers, celery salt, and mustard."

"That is the vilest thing I've ever heard of. The only thing that should be on a hot dog is mustard and sauerkraut," I counter.

"First, pizza, and now, dogs? You're breaking my heart."

Our pizza comes, and we dive in. I hate to admit it, but Chicago-style pizza is delicious. Imagine my shock when I see the sauce is on top, and on the inside is cheesy goodness. Of course, when Ryan tries to get me to admit that Chicago pizza is better than New York's, I refuse.

Inside, I want to tell him that everything is better in Chicago.

Everything.

When we're done with our pizza, we drive to Navy Pier, a 3,300-foot pier on the Chicago shoreline of Lake Michigan, lined with restaurants, shops, tourist attractions, and vendors.

Stepping off the bike, the first thing I see is the 196 foot Ferris wheel I've seen many times from the road, but I have never stepped foot here. We walk under the red sign of Navy Pier Park and head to the Centennial Wheel. The navy-blue gondola of the Ferris wheel is lined with wall-to-wall glass so clear that I feel like I can float through it. We take our seats across from one another.

The car starts to move, and my belly swims with excitement. Looking down, I see the Tilt-a-Whirl ride from a bird's-eye view. As we get higher, I take in the majestic sight of Lake Michigan as it rests against the shoreline of the great city. We reach the highest point on the rotation, and I see far beyond the horizon. Out there, I know the lake touches four states and multiple bodies of water flow its current into the Great Lake.

We make another rotation, and I turn around to see the Chicago skyline. The Willis Tower, the second tallest building in the US, glistens as the sun sets, casting a faint orange on the blue of the windy city. The orange turns to shades of purple, and the night sky is illuminated by the city lights, creating a scene so majestic that my heart skips a beat.

It takes me until the third trip to realize I'm being watched. So enamored by the beauty of the night and lights, I'm surprised to see Ryan enamored, not by the view, but by me. The smile on his face and the twinkle in his eye make the third rotation more stunning than the first two.

The ride ends, and we stroll through the pier, walking hand in hand so as not to lose each other in the crowd. When we hear music pouring out from the Landshark Beer Garden, Ryan tugs on my hand, and together, we dance.

We dance like fools, and our laughter is contagious.

We dance like lovers, and our movements are empowered.

We dance like two rivers flowing into one another.

Walking and talking, we explore the pier, passing boat rentals and more restaurants. We pass vendors and the hall that's made to resemble Atlantic City.

He guides me to the carousel, and I choose a golden horse with its head held high in the air and a blue saddle. It's the first time I've ever been on a carousel, and I adore it. Love it. Will cherish it forever.

As we exit the pier, he guides me away from the parking lot and up to Michigan Avenue.

"This is my favorite street in the whole city," I say, looking up at Nordstrom.

"Fancy shops for a fancy girl."

"Yes, and no," I say. "Okay, mostly yes, but it's also so beautiful with the way it lights up at night. It's so clean and welcoming. They don't call it the Magnificent Mile for nothing."

"No, they don't." He stops at the sight of a homeless man sitting on the sidewalk, his body huddled, despite the warm summer evening. Ryan looks into his wallet and takes out some change, his eighty dollars already spent on our evening. Walking over to the man, he places the small change in the cup and walks away.

I reach into my bag and take out a twenty, offering it to the man. I walk up to Ryan before he sees what I did.

"I've seen you do that before—give money to the homeless. Why?" I ask when we are side by side.

"Just trying to do the right thing." His similar words from the first night we met echo in my head.

"You're all right, Ryan Pierson." I smile at him.

He offers me a raised brow in return. "Just all right?"

I push him in the arm. "Maybe a little more than all right."

We walk in silence for a bit.

Something is lingering under my skin. A bad memory. Unfinished business. I bite my lip and furrow my brow. "I tried to find him."

Ryan stops walking and listens to what I have to say.

"My dad. I hired a private investigator, but he didn't show up. I've been battling my emotions about it. I wanted to make sure he was okay, but I also didn't want him back in my life. When he vanished into thin air, I was relieved. And sad. I'm still trying to decide how I feel."

"You're a good daughter."

"Am I?"

"Yes. You supported him when your only worry should have been where to hide while playing Manhunt or who the cutest boy was in school. Your heart is so big, but you squeeze it tight in your hands. Every once in a while, you open those palms, and the beauty inside shows so bright, I'm blinded."

His words are powerful, provocative, and they scare the hell out of me.

We continue to walk down Michigan Avenue to the entrance of Oak Street Beach. We take our shoes off and bury our feet in the cold sand. It's so odd to me to be on a beach with the city just across the street, skyscrapers looming over where people play volleyball and sun in their bikinis.

It's dark on the beach, but the lights of the nearby roadway give us enough to see in front of us. The soft waves of the lake are singing in the background.

"Who is Maxine?" I ask. I've been wanting to know more about the girl who broke Ryan's heart since his family spoke of her.

"Just an ex." He shuffles his feet in the sand.

"Your family made it seem like you two were pretty serious."

"We had fun, but she wasn't my forever girl. I was upset when she broke up with me. There I was, lying in a hospital, being told I probably wouldn't be able to play ball again, could lose my scholarship and everything—I mean, everything I worked for—and she said she thought our relationship had run its course."

"Ouch." I crunch my face to match my words. "You must still be recovering."

"Not at all. Actually, it taught me exactly what I wanted in a woman. Someone who says exactly what's on her mind. Someone honest. Maybe a little too honest." He stops and looks at me. The twinkle in his eye glistens, as if I'm his someone.

"What's your plan after graduation?" I ask.

"I've been sending my résumé to local news stations around the country. Maybe I'll get a sports reporter gig. Move my way up."

"I can help you get a job," I offer, pulling my hair off my face as it sways in the Chicago wind.

Ryan shakes his head, his hands deep in his pockets. "No, thanks."

"I know a lot of people in the industry. At least let me make sure you don't start off in farm country USA. Get a small city—"

"You'll always think of me as the kid!" he shouts.

My feet halt. When I turn back to him, those cobalt blues are sparkling in the moonlight, his hair getting tousled in the breeze.

"No," I stammer, "I won't."

"Yes, you will. This age thing will forever bother you. The money thing will always eat at you. You're worth more than a lousy ring. You're worth more than a man who is only marrying you out of convenience." His body is strong and commanding, towering over me in a way that reads red-blooded male.

"Why would you say that?"

"I have eyes. He doesn't look at you like you're the most beautiful woman he's ever seen. He doesn't smile at the sound of your voice or wonder how in the world he landed a girl so damn smart and sassy and sexy. He doesn't look at you like he wants to spend forever with you."

I swallow. The deepness of his voice and the power of his words make the blood in my body run so hot that I might burn from the inside out.

"What does that look like?" I'm not sure my heart has ever pounded this hard in my life.

"Like the way I'm looking at you right now."

Ryan leans forward and runs his hand into my hair, and with aggressive desire, he kisses me like I've never been kissed before. His warm lips entwine with mine. His tongue is hot against my own. I swear, we both might ignite.

I lift my arms and hold him tight, getting lost in the peppermint of his breath and the smell of the lake and evening fog.

We kiss in the moonlight, our bodies becoming one, and we can't get close enough, can't feel enough of each other. Every taste and each sensation is more powerful with every swipe of the tongue and dance of the lips.

We are two currents crashing into one another. My current is flowing so strong through my body that I can't control the storm inside me.

We kiss for a moment.

We kiss for eternity.

We kiss beyond the horizon.

"Take a chance on me," Ryan says, his hands still on me, his forehead pressed hard against my own. "Be with me, Heather," he pleads. "Let me show you how wonderful this world can be. Let me be your home."

Home.

I've never known a home before I met Ryan. I've never felt love before I found him.

I close my eyes and try to fight off the insecurities. "I want to, Ryan. I just…"

"You're scared," he says. His words reek of desperation and determination.

"Petrified." I open my eyes and look up into his, those eyes the color of the most beautiful waters of the world.

"Nothing in this world is worth doing unless it scares you a little."

He kisses me again, and I fall into him. Not wanting to let go. Not wanting this moment to cease.

Flashbacks of a childhood I never asked for haunt my mind. Of being locked in my room so that I wouldn't get in the way. Waking up in the morning to no food in the house. Going to school and being laughed at for my ragged appearance. Stealing and getting arrested at twelve years old and then getting hit by my father for being stupid enough to get caught. Running away from home and sleeping in my car at sixteen. Showering in the locker room before anyone knew I didn't have a place to live. Working three shifts while in college so that I could afford braces. Transforming my life, becoming like the women I idolized on TV.

Not wanting to be my father. Not wanting to be my mother.

Swearing to never let a man destroy me again. Making sure I not only had money, but also making sure I'd never have to worry about it again.

I was never going back.

And, in the end, what have I become?

A cold, heartless woman who seeks out men for money.

I hate who I am.

Ryan looks at me like I am something special. But I'm not. He deserves more. He deserves someone who has love in her heart, someone who didn't connive others in order to get to where she is today.

He deserves better.

"I'm sorry, Ryan." I step back and shake off the remorse I feel for everything I've put him through. "I shouldn't have come out tonight."

His face falls, his eyes wide with panic. "Don't do this, Heather. We're supposed to be together. I know you feel it."

He takes a step toward me, and I take three steps further back, my hands stretched out in front of me. His eyes redden with tears he doesn't allow to fall.

"I love you, Heather."

My breath gets caught in my lungs. I can't breathe. My chest is constricted, my body cold as steel. No one has ever said those words to me before, and I vow to make his the last I hear.

"I wish I could say the same."

I walk away, leaving Ryan alone on a darkened beach.

I walk away from his arms, the first place I ever felt at home.

Bless me, Father, for I have sinned.

I just lied to the first man I've ever loved.

chapter EIGHT

"Heather, love, come on in."

I walk into Jarrod's office and close the door behind me. He's awfully chipper for a Monday morning.

Or perhaps I'm just glum.

Not getting out of bed all day, watching heartbreaking romance movies, made for a poor excuse of a Sunday. I only watched films where one of the main characters would die— *Love Story*, *The English Patient*, *Titanic*, *Ghost*, *West Side Story*. I had to put extra hemorrhoid ointment on the bags under my eyes to contain the puffiness that followed after a day of ugly crying.

Looking at Jarrod at his desk, the same desk I caught him screwing Misty Waters on a month ago, makes me ill.

"You told Meg you needed me to review something." I want to get to work and get on with my life.

Jarrod's handsome face looks over to me, taking in my appearance. "You look like something the cat dragged in. Where's my always put-together fiancée? Now that we're engaged, I expect you to be dressed to the nines. And this"— he motions to my face that is splotchy from a day of crying over love stories—"is not the woman who is to be my wife."

"Maybe you should make it a part of the prenup," I mumble.

"That's not a bad idea," he says.

I snap out of my stupor.

"I'll call my attorney and have it added. Here, take a look."

I take the document from Jarrod's hand and skim the text. If I am caught cheating or stealing from him, I will be cut loose without a penny. If I publicly embarrass him in a way that leads to social or legal retribution, then I'll walk away with half a million dollars, but I'll lose that if I void the attached nondisclosure agreement. If I can't bear children, I'll get a million as a peace offering. And should Jarrod decide the marriage has come to an end, I will accept the divorce without contest, and I will receive two million dollars for my time.

Jarrod said he didn't plan to divorce, but if he did, the money I'd walk away with is staggering. Yes, while this might seem like a reward for marrying someone I don't love, it's actually a punishment. It's as if Jarrod has already planned on me screwing up his life in some way. And, if I don't, he has a plan should he just be done with me.

It's degrading. Yes, I only wanted to marry him for his money, but I was still planning on being a good wife, on working hard and supporting him, as any wife would.

"You're no better than he is," I say, my head spinning with comparisons between Jarrod and my father.

"Than who?" He leans back in his chair, curiosity written all over his face.

"My father." I back away, taking a step toward the door.

"You have a father?" He seems genuinely surprised.

I've never spoken of my parents to him. He probably assumed they were dead.

I take another step back, closer to the door.

Jarrod sees my steps. His brows dramatically curve in. "Where are you going, love?"

"If I marry, it will be to someone who is crazy about me and who I am absolutely, without a doubt, crazy over." I open the door and step into the doorway.

Jarrod is on his feet. "What the hell are you talking about? Heather, is there someone else?"

I look down for a moment and grin to myself. "There is. And he is way too young and probably comes with college loans." I lift my head and smile so bright at Jarrod that he probably thinks I've lost my mind.

"College?" His eyes are bulging out of his head. "Have you gone mad?"

"Yes, I think I have."

Closing the door behind me, I run down the hallway and toward the newsroom. I look for Ryan. His intern desk is neat, looking untouched for the day. I spin around the room but don't see him.

He's not in the conference room or the break room. Hell, he's not even in the copy room.

"Meg"—I surprise her with my rushed appearance—"have you seen Ryan?"

She peers up from her red rims. "You mean, the intern?"

I enthusiastically nod my head.

"He quit," she says.

My stomach drops.

"Gave his notice in an email this morning. You didn't see the memo?"

No, I didn't. But it doesn't matter.

"Cancel all my appointments," I say, rushing down the hallway toward the elevator.

Meg peeks her head out of the doorframe, shouting toward me, "Where are you going?"

I turn around and walk backward, feet from the elevator bank. "I have to return a pair of shoes!"

As I wait on Michigan Avenue, my eyes are looking straight at Lake Michigan, the most beautiful lake in the world.

I see a man, the man I've been waiting to exit a building for the last fifty minutes. He's in a button-down shirt and khaki pants, and a brown messenger bag is slung over his shoulder.

A taxi pulls to the curb, and I pause a second before rushing up. The man's hand is already on the handle as I come up behind him and place my hand on top of his.

"I hailed this cab first. Why is it that every woman in Chicago thinks—" His words are cut off at the sight of me.

"Every woman in Chicago what?" I ask with a teasing smile.

Cobalt blues shine in surprise. I raise my brows, and my smile follow suit as I trace the petals of a lavender rose across my lips.

Ryan's body sinks back in surrender. "Heather," he whispers my name. "This is either a crazy coincidence, or you're stalking me."

"I'm stalking you. Well, I cyberstalked your sister, who gladly told me you had an interview here today."

I lower the rose and hand it to him. Our fingers touch with the handoff, and it takes everything out of me not to grab ahold of him and pull his body toward mine.

"I forgot to tell you something." I bite my lip and pray I didn't mess everything up last night. "I'm in love with you."

He looks up to the sky, closes his eyes, and takes a couple of quick breaths. It's not the reaction I was hoping for.

When he lowers his gaze, his face looks like that of a man torn. "That's what you say today. You've already pushed me away twice. I'm still ten years younger than you. I'm still from a working-class family. Hell, I won't be able to support you for at least another five years."

"I'll support you," I reply quickly.

His head swivels to the side in disbelief.

The cab driver barks from inside the cab, "I can't sit here. I have to move."

Placing a hand on Ryan's arm, I move him away from the car and let the cab leave. We have things to discuss, and I am not letting him out of my sight until he hears me out.

"I've spent my whole life looking after me and only me. I thought the only man worth having would be one who could take care of me financially. But that's not what I need. I need you, Ryan. I need to laugh and dance and play games. I make enough money to support us. But what I don't have is someone to support me with his heart, with his mind, and with his soul. You are the only man worth having. The only man I ever want to have for the rest of my life."

The breath escapes Ryan's chest. His body steps toward me, and those hands I adore grab ahold of me. "I want this. So bad. How do I know you won't change your mind, tell me you're scared of the age difference or how we can't live the lifestyle you want?"

Placing my hand in my tote bag, I take out a pair of boring brown loafers. "Because I was only to return these when I was safe. I'm safe, Ryan. With you. Only you."

A laugh escapes his lips. A magnificent, boisterous laugh.

Ryan leans in and kisses me, hard, passionately, and like a man who is kissing a woman he knows he is about to spend forever with.

The petals in the rose in his hand tickle the side of my face. I lean back and look into his beautiful young face.

"Do you know why I chose lavender?" he asks.

I shake my head. "No." I never thought there was a reason.

He pulls me toward him, and his lips speak against mine, "It means, love at first sight."

I kiss him again, on a busy street in Chicago.

In a city where I came to find a place to belong, instead, I found a home.

A life.

A love.

I'd call that a win for a sin.

MORE BOOKS BY JEANNINE COLETTE

THE ABANDON COLLECTION

Pure Abandon
Reckless Abandon
Wild Abandon
Wild Abandon Christmas
Sinful Abandon
True Abandon

STAND-ALONES

Wrecked
A Really Bad Idea
Just Ten Seconds

THE SEXTON BROTHERS NOVELS
(CO-WRITTEN WITH LAUREN RUNOW)

Austin
Bryce
Tanner

COCKY HERO CLUB
(CO-WRITTEN WITH LAUREN RUNOW)

Layover Lover

KEEP IN TOUCH

www.jeanninecolette.com

www.facebook.com/groups/1671316156434656/

www.facebook.com/JeannineColetteBooks

www.instagram.com/jeanninecolette/

https://twitter.com/jeanninecolett

https://www.bookbub.com/profile/jeannine-colette

https://www.goodreads.com/author/show/13931286.
Jeannine_Colette

https://bookandmainbites.com/JeannineColette

ACKNOWLEDGMENTS

A year ago, I was asked to join this incredible group of authors, many of whom I did not know before. Thank you to Carina Adams, Leddy Harper, Nicole Hart, Lauren Runow, Stephie Walls, and SL Ziegler for being the greatest friends and collaborators an indie author could ask for. I love you TWOTs!!!

To my beta babes—Lauren Runow, Stefanie Pace, Kelli Mummert, and Giovanna Bovenzi Cruz—for helping make *Sinful Abandon* an amazing read.

To Jovana Shirley of Unforeseen Editing for always making my stories glow beautifully on the page.

To Autumn Hull for always being my final set of eyes.

To Emily Smith Kidman for helping share the Abandon Collection with readers.

To Meg Rhea and Michaela Duarte, who won a Facebook contest and let me name characters after them.

I only write about cities I've traveled to, but I always need a local to give it that authentic feel. Thank you, Sarita Bernal Woerheide, for being my guide and helping to make Chicago come to life.

To my mom for her time and to my kids for their patience.

And to Bryan for always telling me what a man would *really* say. ;)

ABOUT THE AUTHOR

Jeannine Colette combines humor and angst in her sexy, stand-alone romance novels. Her stories feature dynamic heroines and swoonworthy heroes, who have to *abandon their reality* in order to discover themselves...and love along the way.

A graduate of Wagner College and the New York Film Academy, Jeannine went on to become a Segment Producer at CBS News and NBC. She left the television industry to focus on her children and pursue a full-time writing career. She lives in New York with her husband, the three tiny people she adores more than life itself, and a rescue pup named Wrigley.